Greetings, iCarly fans!

Hey iCarly fans, it's Carly again! We have just hit another milestone for iCarly – my live fight with Shelby Marx. Not only was the fight streamed on our web show, but it was also shown on cable TV! Moi, pay-per-view, can you believe it? I know, totally awesome!

The idea of fighting the youngest female champ, however, was not so totally awesome and I almost didn't do it. Turn the page to find out what happened and how Neville almost ruined everything – for a change!

Now, I would write more, but Sam is about to come over for dinner (it's Spencer's amazing and 'should-be-famous' spaghetti tacos again!), and I have to help him prep for dinner or there won't be enough for everyone – Sam can eat enough tacos for three! Don't forget to keep watching iCarly! Bye!

SIMON AND SCHUSTER

First published in Great Britain in 2011 by Simon & Schuster UK Ltd,
1st Floor, 222 Gray's Inn Road, London WC1X 8HB
A CBS Company

A CIP catalogue record for this book is available
from the British Library
ISBN 978-0-85707-176-7

10 9 8 7 6 5 4 3 2 1

Printed and bound in Great Britain by CPI Cox & Wyman, Reading,
Berkshire RGI 8EX

www.simonandschuster.co.uk and www.nick.co.uk

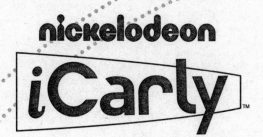

i Fight Shelby Marx

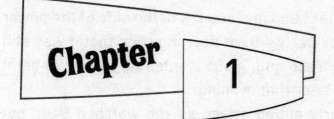

Chapter 1

Carly Shay was in her kitchen preparing snacks. A bowl of crisps and another of pistachio nuts were already sitting on the counter. Carly was pouring a bag of fresh microwave popcorn into a third bowl, and was trying to decide if there was anything else she needed, when there was a knock on the door.

"Open," shouted Carly.

Carly's best friend Sam (short for Samantha) Puckett, opened the door and walked in.

"Hey," she said to Carly.

"Yo-yo!" Carly called back in reply, emptying the rest of the popcorn into her bowl.

Sam looked over at the snacks Carly was preparing. Food was one of Sam's favourite things in the world, and the snacks looked good. She could smell the delicious butter popcorn from where she stood. She spat her wad of gum out into her hand and stuck it to the side of the power box by Carly's front door, figuring that it was still quite fresh and, if she wanted to, she could get it back later that evening.

Carly pulled a face as she watched Sam, but didn't say anything. Carly was used to her bud's habits and knew that some of them could be pretty gross!

"Thanks for letting me watch TV over here," Sam declared, flopping herself down and settling onto the sofa.

"I thought your Mum just bought a huge new TV last month," said Carly. "Wouldn't you rather watch that than my old set?"

"She did," said Sam. "But you know that Senator she's been dating?"

"Uh-huh," replied Carly. Sam's mum always had a new boyfriend, and none of them seemed to have what Carly would call a regular job.

"He stole it," said Sam.

"A Senator stole your TV?" asked Carly, confused. She'd heard her dad talk about crooked Senators before, but she didn't think they resorted to burglary!

"Yeah. Turns out he wasn't a real Senator," Sam explained.

"I told your Mum there was no such state as 'New Kentucky'," said Carly, not sure whether to laugh at this or not. Carly wasn't the best in her class at geography, but she knew her US states pretty well, and New Kentucky had never been one of them, as far as she knew!

"Hey, what's your password to buy a pay-per-view show?" asked Sam, grabbing Carly's TV remote control. Sam and Carly had been best friends for years and Sam often felt more at home in Carly's loft than she did in her own house.

"Why?" asked Carly. "What are we watching?"

"The Shelby Marx fight, of course!" cried Sam. "There's nothing else to watch tonight. I can't believe you even needed to ask."

"Who's Shelby Marx?" asked Carly.

"Uh! Try the best female fighter in the entire Cage Fighting Championship," said Sam, amazed that her best friend hadn't heard of someone so awesome. "And she's only fifteen!"

"We're going to pay to watch two girls fight?" asked Carly. That didn't sound like a great way to pass the evening to her.

"Yeah," said Sam. "So what's your pay-per-view password?"

"Wait a moment," said Carly, trying to slow Sam down. Carly's dad was in the military, assigned to a submarine that at the moment was stationed somewhere near France. While her Dad was at sea Carly lived with her older brother Spencer and he was responsible for all the bills. Spencer was a sculptor, and while Carly thought that her brother's job was totally cool and creative, she knew that sometimes they had to be just a little bit careful about money. Spencer was pretty awesome and would be fine with Carly ordering pay-per-view, but she knew that she should run it by him first.

"I should check with Spencer and make sure it's okay for us to..." Carly started.

"Is the password 1, 2, 3, 4?" asked Sam.

"Yes," sighed Carly, realising there'd be no stopping Sam now.

"Only the most common pay-per-view password in the world. You have to change that soon," Sam grinned. She quickly input the password and purchased the fight, then leant back on the sofa ready for the show to start.

A cheerful knock sounded at the door and Carly's friend and neighbour Freddie Benson walked in.

"Hey," he said to the girls. "Do you want to work on..."

"No!" Sam interrupted him. "Whatever you want, we can't do it. Stop talking."

"Why?" Freddie asked, wondering if he had done anything in particular to upset Sam this time.

"Because you never say anything interesting," complained Sam. Freddie and Sam never got on, and Carly spent most of her time trying to stop arguments between the two of them. Freddie just got on Sam's nerves. She couldn't help it. She just found him super annoying. Plus he had had this stupid crush on Carly, since, like, forever. He just wouldn't face up to the fact that Carly wasn't interested in him and that bugged Sam most of all.

"Now sshhh!" she told him.

"What's the deal?" asked Freddie, ignoring Sam and walking into the kitchen to talk to Carly.

"She's all excited about the Shelby Marx fight,"

Carly explained.

Freddie perked up.

"Shelby Marx is fighting tonight?" he asked, his voice suddenly full of eagerness.

"Has everyone heard about this girl but me?" asked Carly.

"Yeah!" shouted Freddie and Sam together.

Carly picked up the bowls of snacks and carried them to the coffee table near the TV.

"She is crazy hot," said Freddie, and a faraway look came into his eyes. "She could kick me in the face any day."

"Shelby Marx's foot is too good for your face," said Sam. "But I could do it, if you like."

Freddie was trying to think of a smart reply when Spencer walked in from his room.

"Hola muchachas y muchacho," he greeted them in Spanish. He had a rope and a drill in his hand from working on one of his latest pieces of sculpture. Carly knew better than to ask what that was. All of Spencer's art was modern in style and pretty unusual.

"Hey," they all replied.

"Here goes," grinned Sam, pointing at the TV and

turning up the volume. "It's Shelby!" She leaned forward to better see her onscreen heroine.

Pictures of Shelby Marx appeared on TV. She was bouncing up and down in a fighter's warm-up move. Freddie and Carly sat down on the sofa, with Carly choosing the middle in the hope of keeping Sam and Freddie from winding each other up, at least while the fight was on. One-to-one combat might give them too many ideas! On the TV, Shelby was getting some last minute words of advice from her manager. Her long dark hair was pulled back into a tight ponytail, and she was wearing a little black halter top and black gym shorts.

"Man, she is smokin' hot," declared Freddie admiringly.

"She's one mean fighting machine," Sam added.

"Her shorts are so cute," offered Carly, and got unimpressed looks from the other two. "Hey! I admit I don't know much about either fighting or Shelby Marx, but I do know a lot about cute clothes!" she protested.

Spencer sneezed loudly from behind the sofa, but no one paid him any attention.

"Okay, how do I make that girl my future

wife?" asked Freddie as he watched Shelby smile at something her manager had said.

"I thought you wanted me to be your future wife?" remarked Carly. She was pretty sure that she didn't want to be the future Mrs Freddie Benson, but this was the first she had heard of someone replacing her as Freddie's fantasy girl.

"Could that happen?" asked Freddie hopefully.

"Could not happen," replied Carly happily, pleased that Freddie hadn't changed that much after all.

Spencer sneezed again, this time right behind Sam's head. Sam felt something hit her hair and put her hand to the back of her head.

"Dude, you got sneeze goo on the back of my neck! Totally gross!" she cried.

"Sorry," Spencer apologized, grabbing a tissue from a box beside the door.

"You got a cold?" asked Freddie.

"Nah. Allergies," replied Spencer, his voice sounding weird because his nose was bunged-up.

"Bad ones," Carly added. Spencer always got allergies around this time of year. They were pretty hard to live with for a couple of months but then they went away again. Carly was used to it by now.

"Yeah but not after... atishoo! Not after this year," Spencer explained through a sneeze. "You know that doctor who lives in our building?"

"In apartment 7B?" asked Carly.

"Noo!" said Spencer. "The guy in 7B just likes to dress up as a doctor. Promise me you won't ever talk to that weirdo. I meant Dr Dresdin in 10G." Spencer sneezed again, into the tissue.

"He's..."

There was a knock at the front door.

"He's here right now," Spencer finished, sneezing again as he went to open it. A man in a light-coloured sports coat stood in the doorway, holding a packet of tablets.

"Hi Spencer," said Dr Dresdin.

"Hey Doc. Did you bring the medicine?" Spencer asked him.

"Here you go," Dr Dresdin handed Spencer a packet. Inside there was a see-through perforated sheet containing pills.

"Awesome!" said Spencer taking the packet and examining the pills. Half of them were red and half were yellow.

"Now, remember. You have to take them for the full thirty days," explained Dr Dresdin, "and then you should never have allergies again."

"That's amazing!" Carly declared, coming over to take a look at the pills for herself.

"How come everyone with allergies doesn't take this stuff?" asked Freddie from the sofa. "I would, for definite, if I had a problem!"

"Because this medicine was only recently approved for use," explained Dr Dresdin. "Well, not here in the US, but it was approved in a couple of other places," he added.

Carly glanced at Spencer. She thought that sounded worrying.

"Are you sure it's okay for me to... Atishoo!" Spencer began, but couldn't finish his sentence for sneezing.

"I think you should take them," Dr Dresdin advised. "Your symptoms seem pretty bad. But I have to warn you about the side effects."

"What side effects?" asked Carly, concerned.

"Itching, sweating, loss of short-term memory, thirst, muscle spasms," Dr Dresdin said.

"That's a whole lot of side effects!" Spencer declared.

"Do you want to get rid of your allergies?" Dr Dresdin asked him.

"Yes!" said Spencer, sneezing again.

"Then it'll be worth taking the pills," instructed Dr Dresdin.

"Okay. You're the doctor," said Spencer. Then suddenly the thought of the guy in 7B flashed into his head. "You are a doctor, right?" he checked.

"Yes, I am," Dr Dresdin reassured him. "Good luck."

Spencer shut the door as Dr Dresdin left, looking doubtfully at the packet of pills in his hand. Could it really be that easy to cure allergies?

"Okay, everybody. Shut up!" yelled Sam, excitedly from the sofa. "The fight's about to start!"

Carly quickly hurried back to her spot on the sofa between Freddie and Sam. Spencer pulled a stool over to see what everyone was being so eager about.

"Wait. Isn't that channel 3-20-6?" he asked. "That's pay-per-view."

"It's only eighty bucks," said Sam breezily.

"Eighty?" demanded Spencer. That was a lot more than he was happy paying for a show.

"Unless you order it in high-def," said Sam. "Which I did, so it's actually a hundred bucks."

Spencer was stunned at this.

"A hundred b...," he started, only to get 'shushed' by Sam, who didn't want to miss a single second of the fight.

"Here we go!" she yelled excitedly, turning up the volume on the TV.

"Rising star Shelby Marx, at only fifteen years old, is by far the youngest fighter in the CFC division, but no one has beaten her yet," a commentator announced over TV pictures of Shelby Marx preparing herself for the fight.

"True. But that might change," another commentator chipped in. The screen then changed to show another fighter. An older, much stronger-looking girl glared out of the screen. "Tonight, Shelby takes on twenty six year-old champion Maya Feckner."

Spencer sneezed again loudly and Sam turned and glared at him, then ramped up the TV volume again as the referee blew his whistle to signal the start of the action.

"Fight!" the referee called, and the two girls began to circle each other in the ring.

"Come on Shelby!" yelled Sam.

Maya threw a couple of kicks at Shelby, but they missed.

"Take her to the right," shouted Freddie, getting into the action.

"Take her down," encouraged Sam.

Maya threw a punch, but Shelby skilfully ducked it. Shelby then hit back with a high kick that connected, throwing Maya off-balance. She followed through by spinning Maya around and throwing her against the chain-metal cage, which clattered loudly.

"Oooh!" came the cries from the sofa.

"Go Shelby!" Sam yelled again.

Maya then spun around and punched Shelby in the stomach.

"What a hit!" said the commentator.

Shelby recovered quickly, however, and was soon right back in control, landing a kick on Maya.

"Yeah!" cheered Freddie.

As Carly leaned over to take a handful of popcorn Sam leapt towards her, excitedly cheering Shelby on, and made Carly drop half the corn on the floor.

"Go girl!" Sam screamed at the TV, as Shelby delivered a well-timed kick to the back of Maya's legs, knocking her off-balance. Maya toppled to the ground and immediately Shelby was on her, locking Maya's arm and holding her down.

Sam leaped into the air and then bounced up and down on the sofa.

"She's an animal!" she shouted. "I love her!"

"A hundred bucks?" Spencer yelled at the TV screen.

"Feckner in trouble," the TV commentator announced.

"Feckner in trouble!" Sam screamed.

"Shelby's got her in an arm lock," the second commentator explained. Shelby had Maya pinned to the floor of the ring and, however hard the older girl struggled, she didn't seem to be able to move. She had nowhere to go.

Maya tapped her hand against the floor of the ring, signalling she'd had enough and was admitting defeat.

"Feckner taps out and the ref stops it!" the commentator announced.

"It's over?" asked Freddie, amazed at how quickly the fight had ended.

"O-verrrrr!" yelled Sam, still full of energy. She grabbed Spencer for a celebration hug and almost pulled him off his stool.

Back on the screen Shelby Marx was celebrating with her manager and trainer. They were holding her arms up in the air marking her victory.

"Shelby Marx has just shocked the world by becoming the youngest female champion in the history of CFC fighting!" the announcer told the watching audience.

"That's my girl!" said Sam.

"She is so awesome!" said Freddie, as a loud knock sounded at the door.

When Spencer walked over and opened it, Dr Dresdin was standing there with another packet of pills in his hand. He seemed to be slightly out of breath.

"Hey, did you take any of those allergy pills

yet?" he asked.

"No," said Spencer, holding up the pill packet he had been given.

"Phew!" said Dr Dresdin, sounding relieved. "These are the allergy pills." He took back the red and yellow pills he had given Spencer earlier and, instead, handed him an even larger blister pack, this time filled with red, yellow and blue pills. Spencer looked confused and Dr Dresdin had a slightly guilty expression on his face.

"My dog has worms," he explained, backing quickly out of the door and hoping that Spencer woudn't ask any more questions.

Spencer glanced back at Carly, who looked alarmed.

"He gave you worming tablets? Er, do you think you should trust this guy?" she asked.

"Well, I have the right ones now," Spencer pointed out. "Let's just hope the side effects he mentioned won't be too bad..."

Chapter 2

The next night the *iCarly* team were upstairs in Carly's loft shooting another edition of *iCarly*, the live webcast that the team produced once a week. The show was watched by almost everyone at Ridgeway School and by a growing amount of viewers from around the country, not connected to the school.

"Okay," said Carly, addressing the camera. "That completes our five part series on 'Toes with 'fros'."

Part of the reason for *iCarly's* success was the crazy bizarre things that Sam and Carly did on screen. It was really just the sort of stuff that Carly and Sam found funny themselves and thought that their audience would like to see. They were usually right, and their viewers often left messages saying how much they had enjoyed the features. Carly hoped that this week's show would be no different. She was holding Sam's foot out, with the sole towards the camera for the viewers to see. Each of Sam's toes had a happy smiley face drawn on it in pen and then, at the top of each toe, they'd put a mass of fuzzy material that looked like a colourful Afro hairstyle.

Carly released Sam's foot and she stood up next to her best bud.

"Okay," continued Carly. "As you know Sam and I like to keep you up to date on what's cool."

"Soooo," Sam took over. This was part of the way the girls worked together on screen. In fact it was very similar to the way the girls worked together in real life, finishing each other's sentences and continuing where the other left off. "Now we're going to show you the baddest, most butt-kickingest girl in the world," Sam announced, really excited to be able to tell the *iCarly* audience about the new CFC champ.

"Her name is Shelby Marx," Carly explained.

"And if you haven't seen her yet, we're gonna fix that," Sam turned to Freddie, who was behind the camera filming the two friends. "Freddie. Roll the clip."

Freddie kept the camera trained on Sam and Carly while he walked over to his tech cart. Freddie was the technical genius behind *iCarly* and responsible for all their cool clips and effects. He had even come up with the name *iCarly*.

"*iCarly*, as in i - internet, Carly - you," he had suggested and both Carly and Sam had thought it was a great idea. That was pretty amazing because Sam hardly ever liked Freddie's ideas! But even she did have to admit that without Freddie and his technical 'know how' there would be no show.

"Playback," said Freddie as he hit the switch on his tech cart to make the video play to the audience.

The live footage of Carly and Sam cut away to some of the highlights of last night's Shelby Marx fight. Freddie had put together a compilation of the parts of the match that he had thought the audience would like best – the bits that were the most action-packed, and showed Shelby at her most awesome. Carly and Sam watched on from the studio as Shelby skilfully kicked Maya Feckner off balance and then swung her against the metal sides of the cage, as if she weighed nothing. Sam found the action just as entertaining a second time and cheered along.

"Okay," said Carly as the video finished and the camera focussed back on her, live in the studio once again. "Shelby is one seriously-tough chick. Although I have to admit that I didn't know who she was before yesterday's fight, I am pretty impressed with her now, after watching her take Maya Feckner down in less than one round. She looks unbeatable."

"Oh I don't know Carls," said Sam and she giggled. "I think you could take her!" The idea of Carly fighting anyone was highly amusing to Sam, and the thought of her best friend taking on the new female CFC champ was even more ridiculous.

Carly laughed, too. She knew that the idea of her fighting Shelby Marx was completely crazy, but she decided to play along anyway. She leaned in towards the camera.

"Yeah, right," she said in a mock-tough tone."You hear that, Shelby Marx? I could kick your butt. Anytime, anywhere. Let's go Shelby!"

"She's just kidding," Sam cut in quickly, worried that Carly was getting a little carried away.

"T-otally kidding!" Carly added, grinning.

"Carly couldn't beat up my cat," said Sam.

"And her cat only has three legs," added Carly.

"Carly? Not a tough girl," Sam told the audience.

"But I do wear cute skirts!" Carly added. Freddie panned the camera out as Carly did a little twirl, modelling today's outfit – a cute little black pleated skirt with a funky black net tutu underneath.

Early the next morning Carly and Sam were kicking back in Carly's loft, lounging on the sofa. Carly was reading a book and Sam had found the leftover popcorn and crisps from the other night and was doing her best to get rid of them for Carly by eating them. Sam liked to think she was helpful like that!

She had just popped another handful of corn into her mouth when Spencer appeared, rushing into the room from the hallway that led to his bedroom. He was scratching madly at his shirt and jeans.

"Hey girls," he said as he made his way into the kitchen, still clawing at himself. "You guys doing homework? Ooh! Ahh! Oow!"

Carly stared, amazed, then put her book down and made her way over to the kitchen where her brother was now busy opening the kitchen drawers, searching for something.

"What is wrong with you?" she asked.

"Ah. This is what I'm looking for," Spencer said, pulling a long, slotted spoon out of the drawer and beginning to scratch his back with it. The pained look on his face melted to happiness as the spoon helped him to ease some of the itchiness.

"It's just a side effect from those allergy pills I've been taking," he explained. "I've been itchy all day. Ahh, oooh! That's sooo much better." The spoon was helping him reach areas he couldn't scratch otherwise.

"Uh... Maybe you should stop taking those pills for a while," said Carly. "Maybe they haven't been approved in the US yet because the side effects are pretty bad."

"No way am I stopping!" Spencer told her. "I haven't sneezed once since last night. Getting rid of my allergies forever is totally worth a little scratching. Ohhh! My poor itchy thigh!" He worked the spoon down his right trouser leg to better scratch his thigh.

"Don't we use that spoon to cook with?" asked Carly, privately deciding never ever to use it again.

"Uh huh!" said Spencer. "Hey, don't we have a tube of anti-itch cream somewhere?"

"Maybe," Carly told him. "Check the medicine cabinet in the hall bathroom."

"Okay! That might solve my problems," said Spencer, quickly running off to search. As he rushed out of the room, Freddie rushed in. Today he hadn't even bothered to knock. He'd simply flung the door open and headed straight for Carly's computer.

"Hi. Sorry to barge in. Move! Quickly!" he cried, and Carly jumped out of his path. Nothing was stopping Freddie this morning.

He began clicking furiously on the computer keyboard.

"Freddie? What's up?" asked Carly, confused.

"Have you been online?" he asked Carly.

"Not for a few hours," she told him. "Why? What's...?"

"This is bad!" Freddie cut her off as he looking

at the screen, his face serious.

"Aw man," said Sam putting down her popcorn and coming over to see what the fuss was about. "Did someone post more pics of my Mum in her bikini?" It had taken Sam days to get the pictures taken down last time this happened, and a lot longer to erase the images from her mind.

"This is worse," Freddie said, sounding very serious.

That worried Carly. She remembered the pictures of Sam's mum from last time too, and they were pretty bad.

"How could it be worse than the bikini crisis? That was..." she started to ask, but Freddie cut her off again.

"See for yourself," he said, pointing to the screen. He had loaded up the website 'Splashface', where people could share home videos and clips from shows and webcasts they liked. Carly and Sam watched as a clip from their show last night began to play. Someone had loaded it as a video called 'iCarly challenges Shelby Marx' and they had heavily edited it, adding a funky hip-hop backing track.

"You hear that Shelby Marx," said the on-screen Carly. "I could kick your butt. Anytime, anywhere. Let's go Shelby!" Carly didn't seem at all playful, as she had done on the *iCarly* webcast.

"That's so stupid," moaned Carly, rolling her eyes at the video.

"It's dangerous," warned Freddie.

"What are you freaking on about?" asked Sam, amazed that Freddie was taking this so seriously. "Fans re-edit *iCarly* stuff all the time." Sam was always impressed that people liked the show enough to do the re-edits. On occasion she was doubly impressed by the amount of time some of them had taken. Some of those edits were pretty technical and must have taken a lot of effort.

"But people are taking this seriously," explained Freddie, sounding very concerned. "Listen to some of the comments." He scrolled down to the viewer message section underneath the video and read out some of the comments for Sam and Carly.

"That Carly chick is out of her mind," Freddie read.

"Bring on the fight... Shelby would destroy that twig."

"Twig?" asked Sam.

"I'm not a twig!" cried an insulted Carly. "I'm getting curvier every day."

"I know," remarked Freddie, glancing appreciatively at Carly and her 'curves'.

"Eyes up, dude!" Carly warned.

"You're making a big ol' deal out of nothing," insisted Sam. "You shouldn't overreact."

"This video's been viewed almost half a million times," Fred protested. "It is a big deal!"

"So what if lots of people like it?" asked Carly, really not concerned. It was only a video on 'Splashface', after all.

"So what if Shelby Marx sees it?" Freddie asked her.

"Dude, she's a professional fighter," laughed Sam. "She trains, like, ten hours a day." Part of Sam loved the idea that Shelby Marx might watch *iCarly*, or this video and so know who she, Sam Puckett, was. But the other half of her knew that the youngest ever CFC champion had more to think about than a weekly webcast from a Seattle loft apartment.

"Yeah, I seriously doubt she spends her time

watching videos online," Carly echoed Sam's thought.

"But what if someone else shows her and..." Freddie started to try to convince the girls that this video could be a problem, when he hesitated. Something odd had caught his eye. Something really odd! He turned around to see that Spencer had come back into the room. Now Carly's brother was wearing only his boxer shorts and the whole top half of his body and legs were white, covered in the anti-itch cream he had found. Spencer still had the slotted spoon from the kitchen and was scratching his belly with it. Now though, he also had a golf club that he was using to reach his lower back.

"What goes on?" Spencer asked, as if there was nothing out the ordinary about his appearance, or what he was doing.

The *iCarly* team stared at Spencer for a moment, unsure what to say. Then the doorbell rang and saved them all from having to think of anything.

"I'll get it," Carly said, and her day suddenly got even stranger.

On the other side of the front door stood

Shelby Marx, with her manager, Rod, and her trainer, Juan, standing protectively behind her.

"Hi! I'm Shelby Marx," Shelby introduced herself.

Carly glanced around at Sam and Freddie, in total disbelief, and then turned back to Shelby, half-expecting to find that it was all a dream and that Shelby and her crew had disappeared.

They were still there.

"You're Carly, aren't you? I saw your video about me," Shelby told Carly.

"Oh, you did?" asked Carly. She laughed nervously. "That's so cool. Because I..." Then Carly completely lost her nerve. She broke off, turned and ran up the stairs to her room, as fast as her 'twig-like' legs would carry her.

Sam and Freddie stood in stunned silence as Carly run away.

Spencer knew that he had to say something, though he couldn't think quite what was for the best. He walked over to the door, still covered in the white anti-itch cream, and just said what popped into his head.

"Would you mind scratching my back with this

golf club?" he asked Shelby, holding the club out to her.

Shelby and her team looked distinctly unimpressed.

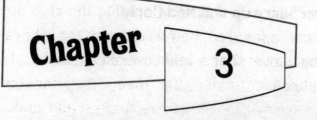

Chapter 3

Ten minutes later there was still no sign of Carly. Shelby and her team were now inside the loft apartment, still waiting to talk to her. Shelby was standing with her trainer, while her manager had made himself comfortable in the kitchen and was sending a text message on his phone. Sam was standing there, too, unsure quite what to do. The whole situation felt really awkward.

"Maybe this wasn't such a great idea," Shelby suggested to her trainer. The girl she had come to see obviously did not want to see her, and she was feeling really uncomfortable. All she wanted to do was leave.

"No!" cried Sam. "This is the best idea ever!" Despite not knowing quite what to say to her heroine, Sam knew that she did not want Shelby Marx to leave. "Spencer!" she yelled up the stairs.

"Will you hurry up and find Carly?"

Spencer appeared halfway down the stairs, still in his boxer shorts and covered in cream.

"I've looked under her bed," he shouted down, "in every closet, on the fire escape and... Oh, that's a big itch!" He started scratching again.

"Just go find Carly!" Sam instructed.

"Okay Okay!" agreed Spencer, running back up the stairs again.

Freddie appeared from the kitchen, carrying a plate which he offered to Shelby.

"Hey Shelby. I made you some raisin bread toast," he told her, holding the plate out hopefully.

"What?" asked Shelby, looking confused and suspicious.

"Pathetic!" muttered Sam. Maybe she should have felt bad for Freddie for making such a big fool of himself, but actually it was kind of funny to see him looking stupid.

"Uh, thanks, but raisins kind of creep me out," Shelby told him.

"Oh," said Freddie. "Well I can get rid of the raisins," he told her eagerly. Freddie picked up the piece of toast and took each of the raisins out

31

of the bread... using his mouth.

Shelby looked on in disgust, but a big smile was breaking out on Sam's face. Freddie was making himself look dumber than she had ever seen him look before.

"Here you go!" said Freddie proudly. "Raisin free!" He held the plate out once more to Shelby.

"You also creep me out," said Shelby, thinking it was probably kinder to be honest with this weird little dude and his toast.

Freddie looked hurt for a moment, but then everyone was distracted by a loud scream from upstairs.

"Ooh, I think Spencer found Carly," Sam announced brightly.

Spencer walked down the stairs with Carly thrown over his shoulder.

"Let me go!" she screamed.

"Just listen to what she has to say," Spencer suggested.

"She's going to punch me in the face," Carly complained.

"No she won't!" Spencer told her.

"You're getting anti-itch cream all over my

32

outfit!" Carly tried.

"It'll wash out. Just relax!" Spencer replied, not giving in.

"Spencer!" Carly screamed, trying to escape as her brother carried her right into the front room.

"Calm down," he insisted.

"Let me go!" Carly pleaded, kicking and struggling as much as she could. Spencer put Carly down in the middle of the room and she immediately tried to make a run for it, but Spencer held on to her firmly.

"Carly," said Shelby in a voice she hoped would calm the girl.

Realising she had no way to escape, Carly turned to Shelby and began to babble very quickly.

"I didn't make that video!" she started. "And I was just kidding around when I said that stuff about being able to kick your butt, but someone took the video and made it look like I really said I could kick your butt, but I don't even want to kick your butt. Your butt's never done anything to me and I'm sure it's super-cute!"

Shelby looked a little overwhelmed by all the information.

33

"Relax!" said Spencer.

"Shelby's not mad at you!" Sam told her.

Carly stopped struggling in Spencer's grip.

"She's not?" she asked.

"No," said Shelby, laughing. "I'm not mad at you."

"Phew," said Carly, letting out a loud sigh of relief. "Okay, good." She relaxed her shoulders and felt much better.

"But I do want to fight you," said Shelby.

Carly panicked again, pushed Spencer against the door to buy herself some time, and shot away up the stairs. Spencer bounced off of the front door and ran after her.

Shelby rolled her eyes, wondering just how long this was going to take.

Juan the trainer walked over to Freddie.

"I do like raisin bread toast," he said.

Freddie wasn't quite sure what to do. He had meant the toast for his new crush Shelby. He most definitely did not have a crush on Juan.

"But why would you want to fight me?" asked Carly, once Spencer had caught her again and she had calmed down.

"Actually it was my manager Rod's idea," Shelby replied, gesturing to Rod, who waved at Carly.

"Oh, well. Thanks a lot, Rod," said Carly.

"Look. We're not talking about a championship fight or anything like that," smiled Rod. "Just a one-round exhibition. Like a show. So you don't need to run away screaming again, OK?"

"A 'show' where Shelby punches and kicks me a lot?" asked Carly.

Shelby laughed. "No. I wouldn't really be trying to hurt you," she said. "Think of it as a 'fun fight'."

"Just a fun fight," repeated Spencer. He was trying to rub the white anti-itch cream off himself with a towel.

Shelby looked at Spencer, puzzled.

"Um why is he..."

"Oh. Spencer is taking an experimental allergy medication," Carly told her,

"Which has side-effects," Sam added.

"Like itching," said Freddie.

"I've totally stopped itching," said Spencer, pleased to be back to normal again.

"Then why don't you put on some jeans?"

suggested Juan. He was sitting on one of the breakfast bar stools in the kitchen, eating raisin bread toast. Freddie had given in and made him some.

"Good call," said Spencer. "Back in two secs." He bundled up his towel and headed down the hallway towards his room.

"This is Juan, my trainer," said Shelby, introducing Juan to Carly.

"Hi," said Carly, giving Juan a little wave.

"I like this raisin toast," said Juan. He turned to Freddie. "Did you put cinnamon on this?"

"Yeah," said Freddie.

"Nice!" said Juan, savouring another bite.

"So, back to this fight thing," said Carly, smiling tightly. "I have to say I'm still not completely sure what we're talking about here."

"Right," said Rod, stepping in to tell Carly the plan. "Shelby's the best young female fighter in the world, but we want more people to know about her. You're famous on the internet."

Here Carly smiled for real. She liked the idea that people other than her, Sam and Freddie thought that she was an internet celebrity.

"But you guys always want more people to watch *iCarly*, right?" Rod continued. Meanwhile Spencer walked back in, now fully dressed, and took a seat listening to the conversation. He was so happy that the terrible itchiness had finally stopped. His sneezing had gone, too! Those pills were good!

"Think about it," Rod continued. "Two famous teenage girls – both beautiful, both successful," Carly liked the way this was going. "You fight it out and millions of people will tune in to watch, which will be a great promotion for both Shelby and *iCarly*."

"I think this sounds awesome!" cried Sam, totally loving the idea. This was her sort of show!

"I love it," sighed Freddie. His two crushes fighting it out... That would be amazing. The only thing that could possibly make it better was if they were really fighting over him.

"But I won't get hurt, right?" asked Carly. The idea sounded great to her in principle, but only as long as there was no pain involved.

"Does it feel hot in here, you guys?" Spencer chipped in. It suddenly seemed to him as if the heating had been switched on, up to the max.

Freddie shook his head. The temperature was fine for him.

"I know I can get this fight booked on primetime TV," Rod said.

"Really?" asked Sam, even more excited.

"No way!" shouted Freddie eagerly. If the fight was shown on primetime TV, it would be almost as if *iCarly* was being advertised. They would get loads more viewers from exposure like that.

"But I won't get hurt, right?" repeated Carly again. Whether it was on the web or primetime TV, she really really didn't want to get hurt.

"No one else is hot?" asked Spencer. He was beginning to sweat right through his t-shirt. Big beads of sweat started to drip down his face. "I'm sure someone must have turned the heating on," he muttered.

Freddie shook his head again, glaring at Spencer and wishing he'd stay quiet about the heating and let Rod go on persuading Carly to agree to his dream fight.

"The fight will make a bunch of money, which we can donate to charity," said Shelby. She even had a charity in mind, which she knew would put the money to good use.

"That's a great idea!" said Rod.

"Yeah perfect!" said Sam.

"Everybody wins," added Freddie.

"But I won't get hurt, right?" asked Carly, a little louder. "Someone say 'right'!"

"Right," said Shelby, laughing.

"No worries," Rod assured her.

"It'll be fine, Carly," Sam started to explain. "A professional fighter knows how to throw punches that look real, but don't actually hurt. Like this..."

Sam turned to Freddie.

"I'm going to hit you," she said, and punched him. It looked like a pretty hard punch that appeared to catch him square in the jaw. Freddie jerked his head back.

"That looked great!" Carly grinned, amazed.

"Ow!" yelled Freddie, grabbing his face. "That actually hurt."

"I'm not a professional," smiled Sam wickedly.

"Shelby, show her," suggested Rod.

Shelby stood up and found a space in the centre

of the room.

"Come here, Carly," she said.

"No," said Carly in a very small voice, trying to back herself as far as she could into the sofa. She saw that Freddie was still rubbing his jaw and that was only from one of Sam's punches. Shelby could hit a whole lot harder that Sam!

"Don't be chicken," Sam insisted, dragging Carly up off the sofa and pushing her towards Shelby.

Carly reluctantly allowed Shelby to position her.

"Okay. Ready?" asked Shelby, getting into her fight stance.

"No," squeaked Carly.

"Yeah, you are," said Shelby, encouragingly.

"Listos!" said Juan. "Vámonos!"

As Juan shouted 'go' in Spanish, Shelby threw several punches and kicks, all in quick succession, and all missing Carly by centimetres.

Carly let out a little whimper or scream as each fist and foot came close to her face, but none of the pretend blows actually touched her. Shelby was much better at fake hitting than Sam was.

Shelby finished her 'attack' with her foot

balanced really close to Carly's nose, so close that Carly could see all the little bits of dirt stuck in the grip on the bottom of Shelby's shoe.

"See?" said Shelby, lowering her leg and standing normally again. "Nothing to worry about."

"So will you do it?" asked Rod eagerly.

Carly thought for a second and then turned to her older brother. He would be the one person in the room who would want what was best for her safety, above what would be good for *iCarly*.

"Spencer, what do you think?" she asked.

"Well as long as it's safe, I think it sounds like a great thing for Shelby and *iCarly*," he told her, his voice sounding strained because he was so very hot. Everyone stared at him. His t-shirt was now soaked and stuck to him. His hair was plastered to his head and sweat was running in rivers down his face.

"What?" he asked. "Do I have something on my face?"

"Um, is sweating one of the side effects of your allergy medicine?" Carly asked him.

"Yeah," said Spencer. "Why? Is it noticeable?"

41

He could feel that he was sweating, but he'd hoped that no one had noticed.

There was silence because nobody quite knew what to say. Spencer looked like a snowman that had been out in the sun for too long!

Later that night Carly and Spencer were sitting on the couch eating soup when a newscast came on TV.

"And it's now official," said the presenter. "Shelby Marx, the new CFC champion, will be fighting in an exhibition match against sassy challenger Carly Shay, the host of her own popular web comedy show, *iCarly*." There were images of Shelby warming up for her fight with Maya Feckner. Then the images changed to show Carly modelling her cute black skirt on her webcast.

"The two girls will be going toe to toe, live on national television, next Saturday night," the host continued, as a promotional image of Carly and Shelby appeared on the screen.

"Wow! This fight is getting a tonne of publicity," said Spencer.

Carly glanced at her brother. He was still soaking wet with sweat.

"You're dripping into your soup," Carly told him.

"Oh, gross!" Spencer groaned, peering at his soup. He picked up a paper towel and mopped his forehead. Then he began to dab the top of the soup.

Carly looked on, amazed.

"I really hope you know what you are doing taking those pills, big bro," she shook her head.

Chapter 4

"I can't believe you bought them," said Carly as she and Sam walked into school the next day.

"They were only a dollar a dozen," Sam explained.

"I know," said Carly. "But I just think it's a bad idea to buy clams from a guy on a street corner."

Sam was always doing crazy things and Carly was used to that. It was part of what made Sam 'Sam' and Carly loved that about her. But sometimes the crazy things Sam did seemed more than a little odd – even for Sam!

As they walked through the corridor, Carly noticed a large poster on the wall advertising her upcoming fight with Shelby Marx.

"Who put up these posters?" she asked, surprised to see herself staring down from the school walls.

"Freddie and I," Sam declared proudly. She

was really excited about the show and wanted everyone to know about it. "We want everyone to watch, right?" she grinned.

"I guess," replied Carly, though in truth she wasn't sure. Although she appeared on computers everywhere via her live weekly webcast, there was something different about millions of people tuning in to watch this fight. Carly was nervous about too many people seeing it. What if something went wrong? Carly wasn't even sure that her friends were allowed to put posters that large up just anywhere in the school.

"But I don't know if you guys ought to be..."

"You're pretty brave, Carly," a tenth grade guy called Will shouted to Carly as he walked by.

"Hope you can take a punch," his friend Grover added.

"No, no. You see, it's just an exhibition fight," Carly shouted after them, but the boys weren't listening. "Shelby's not really going to...,"

"Carly!"

Carly turned around to see her friend Wendy, looking anxious.

"Are you seriously going to fight Shelby Marx?"

Wendy asked. She was more than a little concerned for her friend. She had seen Shelby Marx fight before and didn't know how Carly was going to handle herself against all Shelby's power.

"Yeah, but just for fun," Carly assured her. "It's not going to be, like, real or..."

"Do you know how hard she can punch and kick?" Wendy cut in.

"I know!" Sam chipped in, thrilled to have someone to discuss Shelby's amazing talents. "She knocked out that Russian girl's front teeth with a kick to the jaw."

"I saw that!" said Wendy. "That poor Russian girl."

"Yeah. Now she talks like: 'bwah, bwaah, bwah'." Sam stuck her tongue into her lower lip to make strange noises.

"Can we change the subject?" asked Carly. The conversation was making her nervous. Sure. Shelby had said the fight wouldn't be real, and, sure, she was a professional and knew how to fake a realistic-looking punch, but accidents could still happen...

"Carly," Mr Connick, one of Carly's teachers, came out of a classroom and walked towards her.

"Oh, hi Mr Connick," said Carly.

"Here. Take this," Mr Connick muttered quietly, handing Carly a small, white business card.

"Doctor Rick Shafer?" Carly read out, confused. Why was her teacher giving her some doctor's business card?

"He's my brother-in-law," Mr Connick explained. "Over at St Mary's hospital. He special-ises in facial reconstruction."

"Why are you giving me this?" asked Carly, still puzzled.

"You're fighting Shelby Marx, right?" said Mr Connick.

"Well, yeah," nodded Carly. "But she's not going to smash my face in."

"I don't know," replied Mr Connick seriously. "She knocked that Russian girl's teeth out with one kick to the jaw."

"We were just talking about that!" said Wendy.

"Now she talks like: 'bwah, bwaah, bwah'," said Sam making the strange face and noises again. Wendy joined in, too, with more 'bwah bwaah bwahs'.

"Okay, come with me!" Carly grabbed Sam and

pulled her away from Wendy and Mr Connick.

"What?" asked Sam.

"I'm starting to feel really worried about this whole thing," Carly admitted.

"Why?" asked Sam.

"Oh, I don't know" replied Carly sarcastically. "Maybe it's all the talk about me being punched, and facial reconstruction and some poor girl who says: 'bwah, bwaah, bwah'!"

"Come on! Shelby's not going to hurt you," Sam reassured her best bud. "She said so, didn't she?"

"What if she forgets?" asked Carly.

"She's a professional," said Sam. "You're going to be totally safe."

Carly nodded and started walking after Sam towards their class when her phone beeped to let her know that she had a new message. She flipped her phone open to see who it was from.

"Who texted you?" asked Sam. "I'm hoping it wasn't Freddie with one of his cutesy little sick-making messages."

"It was Shelby's manager," said Carly. "The press conference is tomorrow night."

"Ooh, that reminds me," said Sam. "I've got to

teach you how to trash talk!"

"Trash talk?" asked Carly.

"Yeah! You and Shelby have to get in each other's faces at the press conference," said Sam, "and say mean stuff and pretend you hate each other."

"Why?" asked Carly. She didn't hate Shelby. In fact she thought she was totally cool, and as far as she knew Shelby didn't hate her either.

"Because it gets people all psyched up to watch the fight!" said Sam.

"But I don't think I'm the trash talking type," sighed Carly. It was true that she didn't really like to say mean things about people at all.

"Well try," said Sam. "Ok, pretend I'm Shelby. Now say something to get me mad."

Carly thought for a moment and tried to put herself in a 'mean' frame of mind.

"Hey," she sneered, feeling that she had started well. "You wanna piece of me? Well too bad. Er... No pieces for you!" Now it wasn't going so well. "Jerk!" she added quickly on the end.

Carly looked expectantly at Sam, who did not look at all impressed with Carly's first attempt.

"We'll work on it," Sam said kindly. It would take a miracle to make Carly seem any harder than a marshmallow.

The following night Carly arrived at the hotel for the press conference with Sam, Freddie and Spencer there to support her. Spencer had finished the sweating phase of his allergy med side effects. Now he had moved on to something else.

"Thirsty. So thirsty!" he cried, hurrying the others into the conference room. A long table ran the width of the room and behind it were two large posters – one of Carly and one of Shelby Marx in her fight gear, looking awesomely tough.

"We sit this side, in front of the Carly poster," said Freddie.

"Oh, thank God. Water!" whimpered Spencer, grabbing the tiny water bottles that had been placed in front of each chair and drinking them all, one after the other.

"What's his problem now?" Sam asked Carly.

"Another side-effect, I think," Carly explained.

"Well, at least his sweating stopped," said

Freddie, trying to put things in a positive light.

"Yeah, but now he's insanely thirsty," said Carly. "He's been drinking water like that ever since he woke up this morning."

"Is that why he tried to drink that puddle outside?" asked Sam.

Carly nodded as Spencer finished off the last of the mini water bottles. He spotted a hotel employee and called him over.

"Hey, buddy. I'm going to need some more of these," he told him, holding out an armful of water bottles.

The employee gave Spencer a weird look.

"Look. They're empty, and I'm desperate," Spencer said, and one-by-one he shook the bottles upside down and caught the drips in his mouth.

"Here comes Team Shelby," Freddie announced.

Shelby, Rod and Juan walked in accompanied by an older lady, who must have been in her late seventies or early eighties.

"Okay. Remember the trash talk," Sam said quietly to Carly.

As the chairs on the other side of the table

filled up with members of the press, Rod stepped up to the podium and cleared his throat.

"Hi," he addressed the crowd. "I'm Rod Springer and I'm pleased to welcome you all here tonight so we can talk a little bit about our two fighters – Carly Shay," Carly gave everyone watching a little wave, "and, of course, Shelby Marx." Rod paused to allow applause for Shelby.

The hotel employee had returned with dozens of bottles of water for Spencer, who piled them on to the table in front of him.

"But first," Rod continued. "I'd just like to welcome a special guest, Shelby's grandmother Edith, who just got home from hospital yesterday and is here to support Shelby. Wave to the people, Edith!"

Edith waved at the cameras as Shelby put her arm around her grandmother and hugged her, smiling happily.

"Okay, Carly," said Rod turning to the other side of the table. "Why don't you come up here first?"

"Um, sure," said Carly, getting up from her seat.

"Trash talk!" Sam whispered as Carly moved towards the podium.

52

"Okay!" Carly whispered back. She smiled at Rod as she reached the podium and then took the microphone from him.

"Hi, I just want to say that I'm really looking forward to getting in that cage and, you know, mixing it up with Shelby." Carly made little punching moves as she said this last part.

Sam shook her head. Carly sounded really lame. Catching Carly's eye, she made stronger punching motions and mouthed what Carly should say next.

"Oh," said Carly, reading Sam's lips, "and I'm going to give her a good pop in the mouth!"

Everyone looked slightly confused on Shelby's side of the table.

Sam was appalled. Even when she told Carly what to say, it came out sounding dumb.

"Questions?" asked Carly, nervously.

"Over here!" shouted all the reporters at once, putting their hands into the air. Carly nervously pointed at a reporter in the front row, who stood up and asked a question.

"So, Carly," he began. "You've never fought anyone before. What makes you think that you can take on a great fighter like Shelby Marx?"

"Ah, good question," said Carly, who had no idea what to say. "Um..." she glanced over at Sam for help, who mouthed the words 'trash talk' to her again.

"Well, you call Shelby a great fighter," said Carly, trying to think on her feet. "But I say she's just a punk!" Shelby looked shocked at this. She hadn't been expecting Carly to run her down.

Sam was pleased, though. Judging from the murmuring and 'ooh's' around the room, the press liked that 'sound bite'.

"And not the cool kind!" Carly added.

Sam shook her head. Carly had to ruin it.

"Carly!" called a reporter from the back of the room.

"Yeah, question?" asked Carly, feeling more confident with her answering now.

"Are you saying that you don't respect Shelby's punching and kicking power?" he asked.

"Oh no, I wasn't saying..." Carly began to answer in her standard polite way, but then she heard Sam cough loudly and meaningfully to urge her on with the 'trash talk'.

"I mean... yes," Carly tried again.

Sam had had enough of this. Carly might be her best bud in the entire world, but she was making a terrible mess of the trash talk. She stood up and hurried over to join Carly at the podium, snatching the microphone.

"Carly meant to say that she's not scared of Shelby Marx because Shelby's not even that good a fighter," said Sam. "She's all hype."

Now Shelby was really shocked. Why would these girls say something like that?

"Don't over-do it!" Carly whispered to Sam. The crowd were making astonished noises and Carly was getting worried that Sam was a little too good at insulting.

"We don't want to upset anyone!" she whispered.

"Don't worry. I've got this," Sam whispered back.

"In fact," Sam told the press. "Carly predicts she'll knock Shelby Marx on her butt in the first thirty seconds of the fight."

The murmuring in the audience got even louder.

"Oh, does she?" asked Shelby, getting up from her seat.

Carly could tell from Shelby's face that she was mad. Hopping mad.

"Well maybe not the first thirty seconds," Carly backtracked, trying to smooth things over.

"Sit down, Shelby," Sam commanded her. "No one wants to hear you run your mouth."

"Are you kidding me?" asked Shelby, to surprised gasps from around the room.

Edith stood up, placing herself between Shelby and Sam.

"Don't you talk to my granddaughter like that," she said.

"Sit down, old lady!" said Sam.

"I'm pretty sure you're overdoing it," Carly whispered to Sam, smiling nervously at the old lady, who looked livid.

Even Spencer put down his bottle of water and got up from his chair, ready to go over to the girls and stop Sam before she caused any more trouble.

"Okay," said Shelby, really crossly, "if Carly is tough let's go right now."

"Bring it!" said Sam.

Shelby tried to make her way over to Carly, but

Rod and Juan got up to hold her back.

On the other side of the table, Sam was all up for the fight, but Spencer and Freddie tried to restrain her.

The reporters shouted on, trying to ask more questions and also encouraging the girls to go for it straight away and give them a sneak peak of the actual fight.

Team Carly and Team Shelby ended up in the middle behind the podium, Carly was doing her best to keep out of everyone's way – particularly Shelby's. From the look in the CFC champion's eyes she wanted to hit Carly the way she had that poor Russian girl who ended up with the unfortunate 'bwah, bwaah, bwahs'!

"I'm sorry! I didn't mean it!" Carly was shouting, but nobody could hear her above the noise of everyone else talking loudly. Shelby's grandmother, Edith, was right in Carly's face, waving her finger and telling Carly off. Carly couldn't make out the words, but she knew Edith was giving her a lecture.

She tried again to explain to the old lady that it was just for fun.

"None of what we said was for real," she explained, but it was no good. Then all of a sudden someone pushed someone, who knocked someone else. The next think Carly knew she was tumbling into the podium, along with Edith, and the two of them, plus the heavy wooden podium, were falling to the ground.

The podium cracked loudly under the weight of two people landing on it, and the whole audience gasped loudly at the sight.

"Get her off me! Get her off me!" shouted Edith.

Carly realised that she had landed on top of Edith, and she quickly jumped off of the old lady, a horrified look on her face.

"Unbelievable!" she heard a reporter talking to a TV camera. "Carly Shay just tackled the sickly grandmother of Shelby Marx!"

"Help me! Help!" Edith was shouting, still on the ground.

Shelby grabbed Carly, pulling her up and then holding her by the collar of her dress.

"You tackled my grandmother!" she cried, hardly able to believe it.

"B-but I..." stammered Carly.

"Listen!" yelled Shelby, shaking Carly.

Carly went quiet at once.

"I was going to take it easy on you," said Shelby, her voice calm. "But now you're going down! Hard!"

"Hard?" asked Carly in a small, scared voice.

Shelby shook her once more and then dropped Carly and walked away.

Carly stood glued to the spot with shock, but Sam rushed over to Carly, her face one huge grin.

"That was awesome!" she told Carly. "Shelby looks like she really wants to destroy you!"

"She does!" squeaked Carly.

"Oh," said Sam, the smile disappearing from her face. "Well that's bad."

Before she could say anything else, Spencer noticed a water bottle in Sam's hand. He lunged at it, ripping it from her grasp and emptying the entire contents into his mouth.

"Oh. That's a relief. I could do with some help with these pill side-effects," he sighed.

"You need help?" said a terrified Carly.

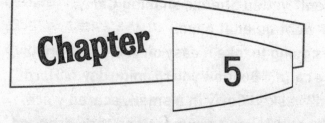

Chapter 5

Carly flew through the door of her loft. She was very, very mad and even more scared.

"You're making too big a deal out if this," said Freddie, trying to calm her down.

Sam and Spencer followed them in. Spencer now had a huge water-cooler sized bottle to drink from.

"No! I'm dead!" Carly told Freddie. "Shelby Marx is going to destroy me!"

"Carly..." tried Sam, but Carly interrupted her.

"Everybody said: 'oh you should fight Shelby Marx - it'll just be for fun'!" she yelled. "Well, it's not fun now, is it? No! Now she hates me, so she's going to punch and kick me in my head until I talk like 'bwah, bwaah, bwah'."

"Well you shouldn't have attacked her grandmother," said Sam, which was exactly the wrong thing to say.

"I didn't attack anyone!" Carly screamed at Sam, poking her friend in the chest to help make her point. "You started a big ruckus with your dumb trash-talking idea!"

The doorbell rang.

"It's Shelby!" shrieked Carly, beside herself with panic. "I'm not here!" She dived over the kitchen counter and hid behind it.

Everyone just stared for a moment, amazed at Carly's acrobatics, and then Spencer opened the door.

It wasn't Shelby Marx but Dr Dresdin standing on the other side.

"You texted?" he asked Spencer, holding his phone in his hand.

Hearing the doctor's voice, Carly relaxed a little, though she poked her head up over the counter first, to check it wasn't some trick. She finally came out from her hiding place when she was sure the coast was clear.

"Hey Doc," said Spencer. "I wanted to talk to you about this allergy medication you gave me." Spencer held up the pack of multi-coloured pills.

"Okay, what?" asked Dr Dresdin, sounding

annoyed to have been called here.

"First I was itching like crazy," Spencer explained. "Then I was sweating like an animal and now I'm insanely thirsty, no matter how much water I drink." Spencer waved his giant water bottle at Dr Dresdin.

"I told you," the doctor said. "To get rid of your allergies forever, you're going to have to put up with some side effects."

"Okay," said Spencer. "But are you sure these pills are safe?"

"Man, you ask a lot of questions," Dr Dresdin said with a sigh.

"Hey you guys, we're on the news!" Sam announced to the others.

Carly and Freddie hurried over and joined Sam on the sofa.

"Turn it up," Freddie told her.

Spencer and Dr Dresdin moved in from the doorway so that they could see the TV too.

"But the press conference erupted in chaos," read the TV news reporter, "when Carly Shay tackled the elderly grandmother of her opponent, Shelby Marx."

"I didn't tackle her elderly grandmother!" Carly objected. "We were pushed and I fell on her!"

"No need to shout. The audience can't hear you," Freddie said to Carly.

The TV then cut to the now familiar footage of Shelby's fight with Maya Feckner.

"And with Shelby's fighting skills," the TV reporter said, "I sure wouldn't want to be Carly Shay stepping into that cage with her on Saturday night."

"Man," said Dr Dresdin. "That girl is really going to kick your head off."

Everyone stared at him.

"Good luck with your allergy pills," Dr Dresdin told Spencer as he quickly walked back out of the door.

"Thanks," Spencer replied, taking a long swig of his water.

"Well, that's it!" announced Carly. "I'm cancelling the fight."

"Aww!" said Sam, sounding really disappointed.

"I think you have to," said Freddie. As much as he had looked forward to his two crushes fighting, he didn't want his major crush to get her teeth kicked in. She wouldn't look half as pretty then.

"Agreed," said Spencer, pulling himself away from his bottle just long enough to get the word out.

There was another knock at the door.

Carly walked over and opened the door to Gibby, a boy who lived in their apartment building.

"What do you want, Gibby?" Carly asked, annoyed.

"Why did you tackle the grandmother?" he asked, shocked. He'd obviously seen the show on TV.

"I didn't!" Carly protested.

"But I saw it," said Gibby, "and it looked to me like you did!"

Carly closed the door on Gibby. She really didn't want to hear another opinion from anyone, ever.

Later that night the *iCarly* team were finishing up another webcast, live from Carly's loft.

"... and that's why garbage cans make really bad underwear," Carly told the camera.

"Right Gibby?" asked Sam.

Freddie panned the camera around to show Gibby inside a metal trash can. It was around his waist, with his hands trapped inside.

Sam knocked on the trash can as she spoke.

"This is so uncomfortable," complained Gibby, waddling out of the frame.

"Well, okay, that's it for *iCarly* tonight," said Carly.

"Uh, except for?" Sam prompted.

"Oh yes," said Carly. "Except for the announcement." She leaned in towards the camera. "I've decided to cancel the fight between me and Shelby Marx."

"Fight's off, people!" said Sam.

"Sorry!" said Carly. "But I've decided I like my face and don't want to see it rearranged. So 'til next time... byeee!"

"Uh-buh-bye!" yelled Sam.

The two friends shouted various goodbyes at the camera as Freddie panned out.

"And we're clear," he told them.

Carly and Sam high-fived each other, pleased with another rockin' webcast.

Hearing that they were no longer live, Gibby walked towards Sam.

"Can I take this thing off now?" he asked.

"Uh, wait one sec," Sam told him, turning to Carly. "Hey, do you think it's possible to give a guy wearing garbage can underpants a wedgie?"

"No. Not possible," Carly and Freddie said together.

"Let's see," said Sam, not one to be easily discouraged.

"No, Sam. No!" cried Gibby as Sam walked around so that she was standing behind him. She grabbed the garbage can handles and began pulling up on them.

"Ow! Ow! It's possible!" shouted Gibby. "Ow! It's very possible! Ow!"

At school, the following day a bunch of students were all gathered around a laptop. They were tuned to 'Splashface' watching an interview Shelby Marx was giving about the fight being cancelled.

"I just can't believe that Carly's backing out of the fight," Shelby told the reporter. "I mean, first she challenges me; then she body slams my grandma and now she just chickens out?"

"It's pretty lame, isn't it?" the reporter asked her.

"Yeah!" said Shelby. "Carly's disappointing all my fans and all her *iCarly* fans. Oh, and the fight was going to raise a lot of money for a good charity," she added.

"To help little animals," the reporter told the audience.

"Uh-huh," agreed Shelby. "We were going to help unwanted bunnies find good, loving homes. But now that Carly's backed out, this little baby has nowhere to go." Shelby held up a picture of a cute lop-eared bunny, which the camera zoomed in on.

"So sad," said the reporter.

The group gathered round the laptop all looked up as Carly walked down the stairs. She was slightly unnerved when she saw their cold looks.

"What's your problem?" Darren, one of the students asked her.

"Huh?" asked Carly, with no idea what he was talking about.

"Why'd you chicken out of the fight?" asked Sheila, a girl from Carly's chemistry class.

"Oh, I didn't 'chicken out'," Carly explained. "I just... I was afraid that Shelby would hurt me so I cancelled because..." she struggled to find the right words, "to make sure that..."

But no matter how Carly put it, it sounded like she had chickened out.

"There's nothing wrong with chickening out once in a while!" she told them.

Sheila shook her head, very unsatisfied with the answer, and she walked off, followed by the other tenth graders.

"Hey dude," said Sam, coming up to Carly. "Everyone's giving me and Freddie a hard time because you backed out of the fight."

"I know," said Carly. "I got called a coward in the parking lot, and those kids just called me a chicken and made me feel bad."

Just then Carly saw Gibby walking past and ran over to him.

"Gibby!" she called. "You get why I had to cancel the fight, don't you?" While he was being forced to wear the trash can underpants the night before, Gibby had also had to listen to Carly's reasoning for cancelling the fight. He still wasn't sure which torture he had found worse.

"Uh, can we talk later?" asked Gibby, his voice

low. "I don't want to be seen with you in public."

Darren walked back along the hallway and looked shock to see Gibby with Carly.

"Gibby!" he called. "Why are you talking to her?"

"I'm not!" Gibby protested. "I was just calling her a chicken." He turned back to Carly. "Bwok, bwok!" he made chicken noises. "Call me later," he whispered to Carly. "Bwok, bwok!" he shouted again, and walked away with Darren.

Carly turned back to Sam, completely shocked.

"Ah, don't let it bug you," said Sam. "Kids can be mean."

Carly nodded as Mr Connick walked past.

"Carly's a chicken," he said. "Bwok, bwok!"

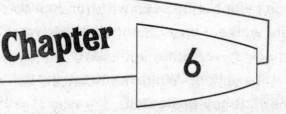

Chapter 6

Carly was really relieved when school was over for the day and she could go home.

"Hi," she said to Spencer as she walked into their loft.

"One sec," Spencer told her. He was on the phone and it had obviously just connected. "Hey Socko," Spencer shouted into the handset. "Happy Birthday, buddy, buddy, buddy!" He then hung up the phone quickly and turned his attention to Carly. "Socko and I always do that on each other's birthday," he explained.

"I know," Carly told her brother. She had made the mistake of answering the phone to Socko one year on Spencer's birthday and getting the message instead. "So, how's your thirst problem?" she asked.

"Gone!" grinned Spencer. He pointed to the packet of tablets on the kitchen worktop. "These pills are awesome. I still have no allergy problems and I think all the crazy side effects are over!"

"Yay!" said Carly, although it was slightly half-hearted. She was pleased for Spencer but she was still totally bummed about the way everyone had treated her today.

"So how was school?" asked Spencer, picking up his phone and dialling it again.

"Bad," said Carly. "Everyone, even the teachers, are calling me a coward for backing out of the fight."

"Aw," said Spencer, about to console Carly, when his phone call connected. "Hey Socko," he shouted into the handset. "Happy birthday, buddy, buddy, buddy!" He then hung up the phone and turned to Carly. "Socko and I always do that on each other's birthday," he told her.

"You do it twice?" Carly asked him.

"No," said Spencer. "That would be a ridiculous idea. So, how was school?"

Carly looked at her brother, now very confused.

"Still bad," she told him. "Um, about your allergy medication ... Wasn't one of the possible side effects short-term memory loss?" she asked.

"Yeah," said Spencer, seemingly not bothered. He put a grape into his mouth. "So, how was school?" he asked her again.

Carly gave a deep sigh. This was going to be a long evening! Just then there was a knock at the door.

"Come in," called Carly, pleased that she might be able to talk to someone who didn't ask her the same question every ten seconds.

"Hey guys," said Freddie as he walked in.

"Hey, is that a new shirt?" Spencer asked him.

"Yeah," said Freddie.

"Nice!" Spencer told him.

"Thanks," said Freddie. Then he turned to Carly. "You been on iCarly.com today?' he asked her.

"No," said Carly. "Why?"

"There have been over a hundred thousand comments in the past twenty-four hours," said Freddie.

"A hundred thousand?" Carly repeated, checking she had heard correctly.

"Yep," Freddie confirmed. "Almost all of them about the fight."

Carly's face fell.

"Let me guess," she said adopting a mocking tone. "'Carly's a chicken', 'Carly's lame', Carly's a coward'."

"Most of them weren't that nice," Freddie warned her.

"Is this nightmare ever going to end?" Carly asked sadly.

"Hey, is that a new shirt?" Spencer said to Freddie.

"Yeah," said Freddie, slightly confused.

"Nice!" said Spencer.

"Okay," said Freddie. He looked at Carly and shrugged.

"Side effect," she explained.

"Ah," said Freddie, understanding.

Carly's phone began to ring. She picked it up and answered it, seeing that it was Sam's number calling. Freddie walked over to the computer on her kitchen worktop.

"Hey," Carly said into the phone. Perhaps Sam could cheer her up.

"Our friend Nevel's been busy," Sam told Carly.

"Oh," said Carly, sensing that this was not going to be a cheery phone call after all. "Now what?"

"Go to Nevelocity.com," Sam instructed Carly.

Nevel ran a weekly webcast but it was nowhere near as popular as *iCarly*, mostly because Nevel's sense of fun was as good as his sense of fashion – ie: really bad! Jealous of the success Carly and her team were having with their show, Nevel never missed an opportunity to try to damage Carly's reputation, or just to say mean things about her. Carly guessed he'd taken his big chance this time.

"Go to Nevelocity.com." Carly told Freddie. She hung up the phone and walked over to get a better look at the screen. Spencer watched too, as Freddie began typing into the address bar.

"So, how was school?" Spencer asked Carly.

"Awesome!" shouted Carly, getting angry. "Thanks for asking!" She turned to Freddie. "So what's on Nevelocity?" she asked, dreading the answer.

"This," said Freddie grimly, cueing up the video Nevel had loaded on his site. Nevel appeared in a chevron-patterned jumper, the type he loved to wear but no other tenth grader would be caught dead in.

"Carly Shay has embarrassed herself yet

again by chickening out of her fight with Shelby Marx," Nevel told his audience. "Oh well. At least you can watch this animated video I've created showing Carly as she truly is. Enjoy."

"Is that a new shirt?" Spencer asked Freddie.

"Shh!" Freddie instructed him as, on screen, Nevel pressed a button and the image of him was replaced by a picture of a live chicken. Nevel had superimposed Carly's head over the chicken's head. The image then became an animation where the Carly/chicken flapped her wings and her mouth opened and shut as she made 'bwok, bwok' noises.

"Okay, that's enough!" shouted Carly. She couldn't take much more of this.

Freddie shut down the video.

"I've got to fix this!" said Carly, starting to pace the room.

"How?" asked Freddie.

"I'm going to fight Shelby," Carly told him.

"You can't!" Freddie reminded her. "You smushed her grandmother. She's going to kill you!"

"Maybe not if I talk to her," Carly suggested. It was her last hope.

"So how was school?" Spencer asked her.

"It blew up, okay?" she blurted out angrily.

"Jeez," said Spencer, taken aback. "Why so temperamental?"

Carly's trip to Shelby's gym didn't go quite as she had planned. When she arrived, Rod led Carly through to see Shelby, but Shelby was in the middle of a practice session with a guy called Gary, who Rod told Carly was Shelby's sparring partner. Shelby was in her usual fighting outfit, whereas Gary was covered head-to-toe in protective gear, and still seemed to be taking quite a beating. Not wanting to stop her training, Rod told Carly to start talking, so Carly did her best to explain everything while Shelby threw perfectly-aimed kicks and punches at Gary.

"And my friend Sam told me I was supposed to trash talk," Carly was explaining, not really sure whether Shelby was listening to her or not. "And then when everyone was yelling and shoving, I just got pushed into your grandmother, and we both just fell over on that podium thing."

Rod nodded as if this was a totally acceptable

explanation to him.

Taking her cue from her manager, Shelby relaxed and turned to Carly.

"You sure?" she asked.

"Absolutely!" said Carly.

"Finish him!" Juan shouted to Shelby.

She picked the pace back up and aimed some more vicious-looking punches at Gary, who toppled over on to the big padded crash mat. Carly looked stunned.

"So what are you saying?" Shelby asked, walking out of the ring and picking up her bottle of water.

"I'm saying I'm really sorry I fell on your grand-mother," said Carly. "But it was an accident."

"Okay," said Shelby after a moment of thought. "I believe you. I'm sorry I got all in your face."

"So ... the fight?" Carly asked her.

"You want to do it?" asked Shelby, pleased but surprised.

"Promise you're not mad at me any more?" asked Carly.

"I promise," said Shelby, laughing.

"And after the fight my face will look pretty

much just like this?" Carly checked.

"Yeah, I'll go easy. No worries," grinned Shelby.

"Okay," said Carly, laughing nervously along with Shelby.

"So we're on?" asked Shelby. "Saturday night." She held her hand out for Carly to shake in confirmation.

"Saturday night," said Carly shaking Shelby's hand.

"I'll let the press know!" said Rod, excited at the prospect of the big fight being back on.

On the practice mat, Gary had pulled off his protective helmet.

"Does anyone have any aspirin?" he asked, trying to pull himself up.

Carly looked at him with sympathy as he rubbed his painful bruises. She felt pleased and relieved that, now she had sorted everything out with Shelby, she wouldn't end up down on the mat like him.

"Phew! That could have been me," she thought.

That night there was a celebration in Carly's

kitchen. Music was playing and Carly and Freddie danced around the table as they set things up ready for dinner. Spencer was at the stove, cooking something but paying more attention to his dance moves than the saucepan on the hob.

"It's open," Carly shouted above the music when she heard a knock on the door. Sam walked in.

"Hey," she said half-walking, half-dancing over to Carly.

"You got my text?" asked Carly, turning the music down slightly so that she could talk to Sam.

"Yeah," Sam told her. "Why are we celebrating?"

"The fight's back on!" Freddie announced.

"No way!" Sam gasped.

"Sure is!" said Carly. "I told Shelby that I never meant to knock her grandmother down and she totally understood, so we made up and the fight's back on."

"And she said she's going to go easy on you?" Sam checked. "She's not gonna pound your face in?"

"Nope!" replied Carly happily. "She promised to leave my face just like this." She pointed to her face with both hands and made a cheesy smile.

"Which is why we're celebrating!" said Freddie.

"With my 'not really famous but magically delicious' spaghetti tacos!" Spencer added.

"Arriba!" shrieked Sam, grabbing a taco and getting into the Mexican mood.

Carly and Freddie cheered as they grabbed their own taco shells.

"Some spaghetti for Carly," said Spencer, walking over to the table with a big bowl of freshly-cooked pasta. He wound the serving fork into the bowl and put a large portion of spaghetti onto Carly's plate.

"Gracias," said Carly.

"De nada," smiled Spencer, "and some for Sam..." Spencer dug the serving fork deep into the bowl.

"Quickly!" said Sam. Everything smelled great and she was totally famished.

"Relax," said Spencer. "Here you g..." As he brought the fork out of the bowl his arm took on a life of it's own. The spaghetti flew into the air and ended up sliding gently down the wall.

"You flung Sam's spaghetti against the door? What's that about?" asked a bewildered Freddie.

Spencer put the fork down quickly and massaged his arm.

"I just had a muscle spasm!" he told them.

"Was that another side effect from your allergy pills?" Carly asked, concerned.

"Oh, yeah. I think you're right!' said Spencer.

"Are you going to be okay?" asked Sam.

"Yeah," Spencer assured her. He picked up the serving fork ready to try serving again. "Now that I know what's going on, I can probably control it."

Spencer loaded up the fork again and was just about to pile the pasta on Sam's plate when another spasm shook his arm. The serving fork whirled around the bowl, out of control, until it shot up into the air. Spaghetti splatted over Freddie's face!

"I can't control it!" shouted Spencer, and he ran out of the room, gripping his badly behaving arm.

Chapter 7

Everyone was happy that the fight was back on. Everyone except Nevel, that is. Across town, he was in his internet 'lair', working on his latest web project, when he heard the news that Carly's promotional contest would take place after all.

"So the two girls have made up and agreed to go forward with the fight," he heard a reporter announce.

Nevel pressed a button on his keyboard to turn the newscast off.

"So, now Shelby and Carly are friends again," he sneered, turning to Mr Tibbals, his large pet porcupine, who was sniffing and snuffling around near his computers. "Well that just won't do, will it Mr Tibbals?" Nevel added, and handed the porcupine a carrot stick. "It looks like Nevel has some work to do." The porcupine munched the carrot happily.

Nevel looked up to where four computer monitors were positioned near the ceiling. "Here we have Carly and Sam at the press conference," he said, cueing up the footage of the press conference. "So now we just need to add some sound, which I can steal from their webshow."

Nevel moved his mouse and brought an old *iCarly* webshow up on to another screen.

"Tell 'em what you did," Carly said from the monitor.

"Well, I went down to see my grandmother," said Sam, "and I took her to Raging Rapids Water Park."

"And made her go down the Mega Slide," Carly told their audience.

"Yeah," said Sam. "I had to push her, but when she got to the bottom she was screaming: 'Again! Again'!" Sam put on her 'old lady' voice for the last bit.

Nevel paused the playback.

"And now with a few audio tricks..." he muttered and reviewed the footage until he found the words he wanted – 'push her', 'grandmother' and 'down'. Nevel then highlighted the audio tracks of Sam

83

saying just those words. "Now we can make Sam say..."

Nevel pressed play on the new audio file he had created.

"Push her ... grandmother ... down," the on-screen Sam appeared to say.

Nevel clicked a few more buttons, removing the pauses between the words and made the phrase sound much smoother.

"Push her grandmother down," Sam said, much more naturally.

"That's better," Nevel told Mr Tibbals, who made some appreciative grunting noises – more for his carrot than Nevel's video editing skills. "Now watch... We clicky. We draggy," grinned Nevel.

Nevel dragged his new audio file to the screen where he had paused the footage of the press conference.

Now when Nevel pressed play, instead of Sam reminding Carly to trash talk, Sam said to Carly: "push her grandmother down."

"I'll do it!" the onscreen Carly replied.

"Wait 'til Shelby Marx sees this," said Nevel.

"Nevel?" his mum called to him from

somewhere else in the house. "Do you have a porcupine in there?"

"No mother!" Nevel shouted back. "Shhh!" he said, turning to Mr Tibbals and giving his pet another carrot stick.

The next day Nevel was ready to put his evil plan into motion and took a trip down to Shelby's gym.

When he arrived Shelby was in the middle of another training session with Gary, who was padded up even more than he had been when Carly visited.

Juan was overseeing the session, while snacking on some raisin bread toast. He had really developed a taste for the stuff!

"Okay, give me an elbow booster again," he instructed Shelby, who obliged, pushing Gary even further against the wall.

"Ugh!" said Gary as Shelby's blow connected.

"Hey, Shelby," said Rod, walking across to the practise ring with a smug-looking Nevel by his side.

Shelby turned around to face her manager.

"What's up?" she asked him.

"This kid says he has something important to talk to you about," Rod told her, pointing to Nevel.

"Indeed I do," said Nevel, who had his laptop tucked under his arm.

Shelby threw a quick kick towards Gary, who collapsed on to the practise mat. Then she walked over to Rod and Nevel.

"Okay, what's so important?" the CFC champion asked Nevel.

"It's about Carly Shay attacking your grandmother," said Nevel, putting extra emphasis on the word 'attacking'.

"Oh, she didn't really attack her," Shelby explained. "It was an accident."

"Was it?" asked Nevel. "Maybe you should see this."

He opened up his laptop as Shelby exchanged a puzzled look with Rod. Even Juan came over to see what this kid had to show Shelby. He brought his raisin bread toast with him.

"Now Shelby," said Nevel. "This is footage from last week's press conference. I was able to boost the audio that so you can hear what Carly and Sam are saying."

"Okay..." said Shelby, a bit confused.

Nevel had now loaded his edited file on to 'Splashface'. He pressed play and the clip began to run.

"What should I do?" Carly asked Sam.

"Push her grandmother down!" Sam instructed.

"I'll do it!" Carly replied.

The video ended and Shelby turned to Rod, stunned by what she had just seen.

"Unbelievable," said Rod.

"So, it wasn't an accident!" said Shelby, her voice full of anger.

"Obviously not," said Nevel. "I suppose you're pretty angry?"

"Uh-huh!" said Shelby.

"Wow," said Nevel, grinning and really pleased with himself." Then I bet you're going to punch and kick Carly extra-powerfully."

"Yeah I am!" snapped Shelby.

"Well, who could blame you," replied Nevel.

Shelby threw her towel down.

"Let's go Gary!" she yelled.

"Oh no," moaned Gary, fearing the worst. Shelby was a terrible opponent when she was in a bad mood. She would show Gary no mercy.

She began kicking and punching Gary with a new energy.

Nevel watched on, cheering from the sidelines. It would be his arch-enemy Carly taking this beating pretty soon.

Finally it was the night of the fight.

At the commentary table Jack and Marvin, the fight commentators, were building up the atmosphere.

"Hello fight fans," said Jack, "and welcome to the Seattle Supercentre."

"Tonight," Marvin took over. "CFC Champion Shelby Marx will be battling it out with internet sensation Carly Shay, from the popular webshow *iCarly*."

"I'm being told that Carly Shay has just emerged from her dressing room and is making her way up here to the stage right now," announced Jack, his hand on his earpiece as he received the message from his producers.

The camera angle changed and showed shots of Carly, Sam, Freddie and Spencer emerging from the tunnel. Team Carly were all wearing matching yellow jackets with the *iCarly* logo on the back, and were cheering and celebrating with the crowd.

"So far there's no sign of Shelby Marx or her..." Jack began.

"Woah!" Marvin cut him off. "Here she comes!"

Shelby appeared from the opposite corner of the auditorium, with Rod and Juan. She was in her usual fight gear, and looked much more professional than Carly did. Instead of waving to the crowd Shelby was in 'the zone', bouncing as she moved, her fists up ready for action.

"Wow," said Freddie, impressed at Shelby's focus.

"She looks pretty intense," agreed Sam.

"Yeah," said Carly. "Hi Shelby!" she shouted, waving to her opponent. "Hey!"

Shelby glared across at Carly. She pointed at her rival and then at the floor, telling Carly that she was 'going down'.

"She looks pretty cheesed off," said Sam, surprised.

"Yeah. I thought you made up with her?" said Spencer.

"I did," said Carly confidently. "She's just acting all tough for the crowd. Here, I'll do it too. Hey Shelby!" she called. Carly then tried her best to return Shelby's mean stare, and even added a little growl. Instead of seeming 'tough' she looked and sounded a bit like a grumpy teddy bear.

Shelby didn't seem impressed by this.

"Pretty scary," said Sam, sarcastically.

"Hey guys," said Gibby, approaching the team carrying a large bucket of popcorn.

"Gibby!" they shouted, pleased that he had made it.

"Man, the popcorn here is awesome!" Gibby told them.

Just then Spencer suffered another muscle spasm in his arm. It flew out of control and knocked right into Gibby's popcorn bucket, sending the fresh corn into the air and all over everyone sitting in the first few rows.

Gibby stared at Spencer as if he was crazy.

"I'm sorry," Spencer apologised.

"I'll go get another one," muttered Gibby, still not quite sure what had happened.

"I'll go with you," said Spencer. "I spilled all

your popcorn so it's only fair I should buy you a replacement bucket."

"Bring me back a root beer!" Sam called after Spencer and Gibby as they walked away.

Spencer waved at her to let her know he had heard.

Sam watched them walk towards the refreshments booth, right past Nevel, who was sitting in the front row. This seemed very odd to Sam. Nevel was hardly going to be there to support Carly now he knew her face wasn't going to get all smushed up.

"Hey," she tapped Carly and Freddie on the shoulder. "Look who's sitting over there."

"Oh wow!" said Carly. "Sir-Mix-a-lot." She thought Sam was pointing out the DJ, not Nevel.

"No! In the front row!" Sam corrected Carly.

"Nevel?" said Carly in surprise. She hadn't expected Nevel to come to see her match.

"Gross," said Freddie.

The *iCarly* team all exchanged looks. Nevel looked very happy, and when that happened something was usually up. They walked over to where Nevel was sitting.

"Oh, hello 'iCarly'. Fancy meeting you here," Nevel said, innocently.

"What are you doing here?" Sam asked.

"Well, I'd heard Carly was going to be fighting Shelby Marx," said Nevel, turning to Carly, "and I thought this would be a wonderful opportunity for me to watch you bleed and cry."

"Sorry," said Carly, "but this is just an exhibition match."

"Just for fun," added Freddie.

The fight bell rang three times, signalling that the fighters needed to be ready.

"Ding, ding, ding!" said Nevel happily. "I think that's for you. Run along!" Still grinning, he waved Carly and her team off. They exchanged suspicious looks as they walked back to the 'Team Carly' corner of the ring, where Gibby and Spencer were already waiting. Spencer handed Sam a large root beer.

Chapter  8

"The Seattle Super Centre welcomes you to this exhibition match between CFC champion Shelby Marx and Carly Shay," Marvin's voice boomed across the auditorium.

"And here comes the main event," added Jack.

The referee blew his whistle and motioned for Carly and Shelby to join him in the centre of the stage.

"You're up, kid!" said Sam.

"Have fun out there," said Freddie.

"Yeah! Make us proud," said Spencer. "And remember to..." His thought got lost as his arm began to spasm once more. It flailed until it found Gibby's new popcorn bucket. As the crazy arm met with the bottom of the bucket, popcorn rained down on them all.

"Dude!" cried Gibby. "Not cool!"

"Sorry!" said Spencer.

"You'd better get out there," Sam said to Carly.

"Okay," said Carly, nodding and bouncing her way to the centre. Shelby and the referee were waiting for her there. Shelby looked all business.

"And here we go!" Marvin said over the loud speaker.

"Hi!" said Carly cheerfully, waving at Shelby.

Shelby said nothing, but glared at Carly.

"Okay girls. This is the main event, and it's showtime," said the referee. "Let's give the millions of fans watching a good fight. Now go back to your corners and let's get ready to rock and roll."

"Cool," Carly told him and then turned back to Shelby. "Hey Shelby. After the fight, do you want to go get smoothies with me, Sam and Freddie?" she asked.

Shelby said nothing, but gave Carly a really filthy look before she turned away and walked back to her corner.

"Ooh!" said Carly, not quite sure what had just happened. Shelby must really get into character for her fights, she thought, as she walked back to her own corner.

"You ready?" Sam asked her.

"Uh-huh," said Carly.

"Mouth open," instructed Freddie.

Carly opened her mouth and Freddie popped in the mouthguard he had been holding.

"Okay kiddo," said Spencer. "Go out there and have some fun."

"I will," Carly told him, although her words were a little muffled because of her mouthguard.

"Now remember. Since this is just an exhibition match it's only scheduled for one three-minute round," Jack told the audience.

"But no one's ever lasted a full round with Shelby Marx, so I doubt that even matters," said Marvin.

"Well, thanks for making me feel stupid, Marvin," said Jack, a little put out that he had been corrected in front of the whole Super Centre audience.

"You're welcome," replied Marvin.

Back in the ring, the referee stood between Carly and Shelby.

"Fighter, are you ready?" he asked, pointing to Shelby.

Shelby nodded, her gaze fixed on Carly.

"Fighter, are you ready?" he asked Carly.

Carly nodded. She gave the referee a cute salute and began bouncing, as she'd seen Shelby doing on TV.

"Fight!" shouted the referee, clapping his hands to signal the start of the match.

Carly and Shelby began to circle each other. Shelby moved like a pro, whereas Carly continued her bouncing and looked a little awkward. She waved her fists and even pretended to throw a couple of punches towards Shelby.

"Hey, this is kind of fun," she cried, throwing her fists. "Woo! Woo!"

Shelby threw a jab, which just missed Carly's face.

"Oooh!" said Carly, surprised. She hadn't been quite ready for that. "That was close! It almost looked like..."

Carly was going to say that the punch looked almost like it was meant to hit her, when Shelby threw another jab. This time the blow connected with Carly's chin. It certainly did not feel like a 'fake punch'!

"Ow!" cried Carly, feeling her chin where the punch had landed. She stepped back, stunned for a moment, and whipping out her mouthguard.

"I don't think Shelby is just messing around and taking it easy on me," she thought, totally shocked. Suddenly it was clear. For Shelby this match was now for real!

"Time out!" Carly called.

"Time out?" asked Shelby. Now it was her turn to look confused.

"No time outs!" Nevel shouted from the audience. In his opinion this fight was just starting to get good!

"You can't call a time out!" the referee told Carly.

"Well I just did!" Carly told him. Her fear and confusion had made her sassier, and she knew she had to talk to her team to try to work out what was going on.

"Uh, we have an unofficial time out," Marvin told the Super Centre crowd.

Carly quickly walked back to her corner, before the referee could change his mind and make her continue with the match.

"That girl is trying to kill me," she told them.

"I thought she was going to go easy on you?" asked Spencer.

"That's what she said!" Carly cried, totally confused.

"I don't know what she's doing," Shelby's voice carried over from her own corner.

"That makes two of us," thought Carly, as she turned back towards the centre of the stage.

"Let's go!" shouted the referee, blowing his whistle.

Shelby was ready and waiting for Carly.

Carly looked back towards her team, hoping for any last minute suggestions that might help her – and save her face!

"You can do it!" Spencer shouted encouragingly.

"Knock her head off!" shouted Sam.

Realising that she didn't have a choice, Carly turned towards Shelby.

As both girls began circling each other again Carly held her hand up in an attempt to protect her face.

"Hi Shelby," she said, squealing as she ducked

a punch. "Remember how you promised to go easy on me and not really hit me?"

Carly screamed, terrified as another punch missed her head by millimetres.

Shelby raised her leg and tried a roundhouse kick.

Carly ducked under the kick, crouched on the floor and moved towards Shelby, grabbing hold of her leg.

The audience didn't know how to react to this unusual fighting move. Some of them began to cheer, whereas others started to laugh.

Carly was too terrified to notice any of the reaction.

"Let go, Carly! Let go of her leg!" screamed Nevel. He could see that Shelby's blows couldn't reach Carly while she was on the floor.

"What's she doing?" Spencer asked.

Sam shrugged. She had never seen this move used in CFC fighting before.

"Shay is holding on to the left leg of the Champion," Jack announced to the crowd.

"This is very unusual," Marvin added. "I don't think we've seen this technique before."

99

"Let go of my leg!" Shelby shouted. She tried to reach down and punch Carly, but it was very difficult to land a blow on someone curled around your lower leg.

"Never!" said Carly, slapping away Shelby's hands as they tried to grab her.

"Hang on Carls!" shouted Sam.

"Hold on kiddo!" Spencer shouted. "Don't let go!"

"Go Carly!" Freddie added.

The scoreboard flashed thirty seconds. If Carly could hang on for another half a minute the round would be over.

"Marx is trying to shake Shay off her leg," Marvin announced as Shelby hobbled around the ring, with Carly gripping her leg like a limpet.

"She is hanging on for dear life!" said Jack admiringly.

"Is she allowed to do this?" Shelby asked the referee.

"I don't know!" the referee admitted. "I've never seen this move before. As far as I remember, there's nothing in the rulebook about whether it is permitted. Besides, this is an exhibition fight, so I guess the rules are slightly different again."

"Will someone pry this girl off my leg so I can punch her?" Shelby pleaded.

"Carly!" Freddie shouted. "The clock is ticking down. Only ten seconds left in the round."

"Hang on kiddo!" shouted Sam.

"Okay!" Carly called back, clinging as tightly as she could to Shelby's leg.

"Eight more seconds and Carly Shay will be the first girl ever to last a full round with Shelby Marx!" Jack announced.

Freddie looked up at the clock. It had hit the five-second mark.

"In five..." he started.

The arena crowd joined in, counting down the last few seconds of the exhibition match.

"Four... three... two... one!"

The clock clicked to zero and the bell rang, signalling the end of the round.

The crowd cheered loudly. Freddie and Sam clapped and cheering too.

"That's a foul!" Nevel yelled, really disappointed that Carly had escaped with her face in one piece. "Isn't that a foul?" he shouted in rage at the startled girl sitting next to him.

Carly let go of Shelby's leg and ran out of the cage as fast as she could. Spencer held the door open for her, but Carly did not stop to celebrate with her team. She carried on running until she was out of sight of the audience in the arena.

Gibby walked over to the remainder of 'Team Carly' with a new tub of popcorn.

"Oh good. You got some more," said Spencer, with an awkward embarrassed grin. As he spoke another spasm gripped his arm and it flailed madly, knocking the popcorn away from Gibby and into the audience.

Spencer stared horrified as the popcorn flew through the air.

Gibby just looked at Spencer, shaking his head.

"What is your problem?" he asked.

Chapter 9

As the crowd began to leave the auditorium Sam, Spencer and Freddie searched for Carly.

"I don't know where she is," cried Sam, very concerned. "Check down there."

Spencer went ahead, down a flight of stairs towards the main exit.

"Carly!" shouted Sam, calling for her friend.

"Hey Carly," called Freddie. "Maybe she's already gone to the after-show party."

"She's not downstairs," said Spencer coming back up the staircase.

"Aw, man," sighed Freddie.

"Check there," said Sam, pointing Freddie off towards another corridor.

"Guys!" shouted Carly, appearing from behind a large, ornamental pillar. "Over here."

"Yo girl!" cried Spencer, running over and hugging his sister. "Nice fighting."

"You rocked!" said Freddie. "That was a-mazing!"

"Yeah! You rocked, Carls!" Sam agreed, taking her turn to hug her best bud. "You were awesome! You didn't throw one punch or kick, and you looked like a total nerd out there, but at least you went a whole round with a professional fighter. Way to go, kid!"

They all started discussing the fight.

"It was kind of crazy," Carly admitted. "I was just trying to hold on."

Everyone suddenly went quiet as Carly was talking. Eventually she realised they were staring over her shoulder.

"Hey, why is everyone getting all..." Carly turned around to see what her friends were staring at, and found herself looking straight at Shelby. She screamed and quickly ran back behind Sam and Freddie.

"What do you want?" asked Sam, not at all intimidated by the youngest female CFC fighter ever.

"To talk to Carly," said Shelby. "I want to ask her why..."

The muscles in Spencer's arm contracted into a spasm again and his whole arm flailed, slapping Shelby in the face.

Everyone gasped.

"I am so sorry!" said Spencer.

Shelby glared at Spencer, then coolly kicked him with a direct hit to the chest.

"Yow!" said Spencer falling to the floor and clutching his chest. He slowly struggled to his feet. "I'm going to go wait in the car," he croaked, sounding in pain as he headed out of the stadium.

Carly came out from her hiding place and walked over to Shelby.

"What happened tonight?" she asked. "You promised you were going to take it easy on me."

"You promised it was an accident when you tackled my grandmother!" Shelby told her.

"It was," replied Carly.

"Don't lie!" Shelby shouted. "I saw a video and heard you and Sam planning to do it."

"What video?" asked Sam, confused.

"We never planned to do it," Carly told Shelby.

"Are you dating anyone?" asked Freddie.

Shelby glared at Freddie and Sam elbowed him

in the ribs.

"Be quiet!" she hissed.

"All I know is that some kid came to my gym," Shelby explained, "and he had a video showing you guys at the press conference talking about how you were going to push my grandmother down."

Carly and Sam looked at each other with puzzled faces.

"What kid?" asked Sam.

"I don't know," said Shelby. "About this tall." She held her hand up to about her shoulder height. "Our age, round head. Polite, but super-creepy."

Carly, Freddie and Sam all looked as if they'd suddenly realised something important.

"Nevel," they all cried out together.

"Now I get it," said Carly.

"Nevel must have made a fake video," Freddie suggested.

"That little nub!" shouted Sam angrily.

"Maybe he's still here," Carly suggested.

"Go check it out!" Sam suggested to Freddie.

"Right!" said Freddie.

He tapped Gibby on the shoulder. Gibby nodded and the two boys hurried off, hoping to find Nevel before he could leave the stadium.

After they left Carly and Sam stood with Shelby. Shelby was still mad and the situation still seemed awkward.

"Nevel's head is kind of round," said Carly, trying to ease the tension.

"Like a melon," agreed Sam.

Gibby and Freddie found Nevel before he left the stadium. The little nerd had been trying to get himself a souvenir programme at discount price, and they caught him as he was arguing with the souvenir vendor.

Now Freddie was 'escorting' him back to the centre of the auditorium.

"Let me go!" Nevel cried, trying to squirm his way out of Freddie's grasp. "I mean it, Freddie Benson! I have rights! You cannot legally drag me here against my will, or I will drag you into the court house!"

"Alright" said Freddie, releasing his grip on Nevel. "I let go!" He had got Nevel into the cage-fighting area, which is where he wanted him to be.

"I really couldn't stand any more of your

whining, anyway," he said. "Gibby, lights!"

"Lights!" Gibby called back, turning on a spotlight that illuminated Nevel.

"Okay, Freddie," said Nevel, laughing now. "I'm not scared of you."

"That's cool," said Freddie, walking out of the cage and shutting the metal door. He then secured it with the safety chain and leaned against the side of the cage, ready to watch the show.

Another light clicked on, illuminating Carly, who was standing in one of the corners of the cage.

"Hello, Nevel," she said, trying to sound menacing.

"I'm not scared of you either," said Nevel. "I don't know what sort of lame trick this is, but it isn't working."

A third spotlight flicked on and Sam appeared in another corner of the cage.

Nevel's eyes widened at the sight of Sam in her bright yellow 'Team Carly' jacket.

Sam took a step towards Nevel and he flinched slightly.

"What's up, Nevel?" Sam asked.

"Okay," said Nevel, his voice quivering. "You,

I'm scared of."

"Just admit it," said Carly.

"Admit what?" asked Nevel, as if he had no idea what they were talking about.

"That you tricked Shelby Marx with some fake video... " said Sam.

"...that made it look like I meant to tackle her grandmother," added Carly.

"I did no such thing!" said Nevel, doing his best to look shocked and offended at the accusation. Unfortunately for Nevel, he was never going to win an Oscar for acting!

Sam took another step towards Nevel.

"Okay! I tricked Shelby!" Nevel blurted out in fright, taking a step backwards. "So?"

A final spotlight came on, in the final corner of the cage. Shelby stood there, in her fighting gear, pulling her gloves more firmly on to her hands.

"Hi Nevel," she said sweetly.

Nevel spun around to see where the new voice had come from.

"Oh dear," he said as his eyes landed on Shelby.

From his position outside the cage, Freddie grinned as he watched all three girls slowly began to walk forwards towards Nevel, fencing him in.

"Oh, okay!" Nevel said, holding his hands out, trying to keep the girls at what he considered a safe distance. "What are you going to do? Ladies – My trousers are very expensive!"

Nevel screamed as he found himself backed up against the wire with nowhere else to go!

Chapter 10

A few nights later the *iCarly* team were back in Carly's loft making the next webshow.

As Freddie filmed them, Carly and Sam jumped into frame in front of the camera.

"Okay," said Sam. "So most of you guys probably watched Carly fight Shelby Marx on TV a few nights ago."

"But now," Carly took over, "we're really good friends!"

"What?" asked Sam in mock surprise. "You don't believe us?"

"You think I'm lying?" asked Carly in the same tone.

"Well, well," said Sam slyly to the camera.

"Then I guess we'll just have to prove it!" said Carly.

"Get out here Shelby!" they shouted together.

A funky graphic in red, white and blue appeared

on the screen spelling out Shelby's name as the CFC champ walked into shot, her fists up in a 'battle ready' stance. Instead of her fight clothes, Shelby was now in a black leather jacket and a cute purple top.

She hugged Sam as the graphic exploded into fireworks all along the bottom of the screen.

As Shelby moved on and hugged Carly, Sam picked up the remote and pressed a button, which cued cheers, applause and 'whoops' from an imaginary audience.

"No hug for the technical producer?" asked Freddie, hopefully.

"Ok. Come here Freddie!" said Shelby, walking over and hugging him, too.

Freddie turned the camera on himself to make sure he recorded the footage of Shelby Marx hugging him.

Shelby smiled into the close-up shot, but her expression changed as she got a little freaked, realising that Freddie was now sniffing her hair!

Shelby quickly backed up to stand between Carly and Sam, as Freddie turned the camera back onto them.

"Sorry," he mouthed to her quietly.

"Now, how can you be sure that Shelby's really our new best bud?" Carly asked the audience.

"Well, only best buds would do super slow-motion spit takes together," Sam explained.

"With grape juice!" Carly added.

"While a powerful fan blows our hair back!" said Shelby.

"Let's do it!" Carly told the camera.

"Do it!" repeated Sam, as the three girls made their way over to a table.

Freddie had set up three glasses of grape juice ready for them, and each girl picked up a glass.

"Okay, let's get in real close," Sam told Shelby and Carly. "A nice three-shot."

All three of them put their heads really close together, the glasses poises only centimetres from their mouths.

"And ready?" asked Carly.

"Uh-huh!" said Sam.

Shelby looked between the two more experienced co-hosts and waited for her cue.

"Go!" said Carly.

All three girls took a large mouthful of grape juice.

Freddie quickly switched on a large fan and then aimed the camera back at Carly, Sam and Shelby, just as they began to spit the grape juice!

Slowing the feed down for the audience at home, Freddie kept the camera on the girls as grape juice shot out of their mouths and towards him! He had to take a step back to keep the camera lens dry. The fan began to blow the grape juice backwards, and Carly, Sam and Shelby all ended up with juice in their hair.

Freddie switched off the fan, and put the footage back to normal speed.

"Okay," said Carly, once her mouth was empty. "That's it for this *iCarly*."

"Until next time," said Sam, still laughing about the slow motion spitting. She pressed a button on the remote control and a voice boomed in from overhead, announcing 'random dancing'! At the same time a graphic flashed up on the screen saying the same thing.

Sam and Carly looked around them in the air, as if they were trying to see where the voice was coming from.

Then, as Freddie flicked a switch, disco lights

flashed on all through the studio and funky music began to play.

Carly, Sam and Shelby all began dancing and jumping around to the music, as Freddie faded out of the show.

If you enjoyed this *iCarly* story then read all about some other *iCarly* fun in this extract from *iCarly: iGo to Japan*

Hey, peoples!

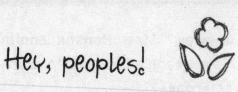

Nanika atta! (That basically means, "What's up, guys!" in Japanese.) Carly here! I'm inviting you to flip through the latest installment in the World iHistory of *iCarly.* That's right, people of Earth, *iCarly* has infiltrated the entire planet—next stop, Jupiter!

Spanning the globe makes for awesome news, and I hope lots of viewers in all different kinds of places are tuning in to *iCarly.* (Imagine what we'd sound like if *iCarly* were translated into other languages. . . . Can you say *"Mademoiselle Carly?"*) Going international was a bit of a challenge. We had to make sure that my brother, Spencer, didn't insult everyone with his language skills (or lack thereof), and that my best friend, Sam, didn't spend the whole time looking for the overseas equivalent of low-fat Fat Cakes (yum!). So grab your passport, and start turning those pages to see how our first international *iCarly* adventure went. And don't forget to check out the amazing pictures, too! I'd write more, but traveling makes me sleepy, especially through different time zones. Did you know Japan is like almost a full day ahead of us here in Seattle? Fluffy pillow, here I come! ☺

Remember to keep watching *iCarly*—bye for now!

Carly

"Anyway," Mrs. Benson continued, "I forgot—this package addressed to *iCarly* came in the mail yesterday—"

Carly stared at her, and at the large, white SendEx box she was holding up. "Yesterday!" she yelped. And she'd been worrying that it had gotten lost somehow!

"I'm sorry!" Mrs. Benson stammered. "I meant to tell Freddie, but—"

Sam ripped the box from her hand and raced toward the kitchen counter. Carly and Freddie took off after her.

"Is that from the iWeb Awards?" Spencer asked as Sam set the package on the counter and the three of them clustered around it.

"Uh-huh, yep!" Carly told him over her shoulder. She'd told her brother all about it, of course—he was her legal guardian, after all. But they were also great friends, and he was *iCarly*'s biggest supporter. No way was she not going to tell him about something that exciting!

"C'mon," Freddie demanded behind her as she opened it and pulled out a bunch of folders and papers, "what country are we goin' to?!"

Carly scanned the papers . . . and her face fell. "Uhhhhh . . ." She looked up at her friends. "Canada."

Sam and Freddie looked at her, and at each other.

"Canada?" Sam repeated. They lived in Seattle! Canada was right over the border! They could go there anytime!

Carly let them suffer for a few seconds more before she broke into a big smile. "Just kiddin'— TOKYO! We're goin' to JAPAN!"

Sam started screaming, and Freddie and Carly joined in. They jumped around and high-fived and hugged each other.

"Uh, Freddie, you can let go now," Carly reminded him after his hug lasted a little too long.

"Oh, right." He let her go and stepped back a bit.

Spencer was looking at the information from the package. "Sweet!" he said. "Y'know, I took a year of Japanese in college. A little brush up and I'll be speakin' Japanese like a"—he paused, searching for the right word—"Japanesiologist." Carly's brother never let his lack of knowledge stop him. Ever.

Mrs. Benson didn't look too happy, however. She snatched the papers from Spencer and glanced at them. "Freddie, I'm not sure I can allow this," she warned.

"Here we go," Sam sighed. She wasn't particularly fond of Freddie's mother.

Right now, Freddie wasn't happy with her either. "Mom!" he protested.

"It's just Japan," Carly tried to assure her. But for Mrs. Benson, worrying too much was a way of life.

"Right," she told Carly, "which is why I worry that . . . y'know, the Far East can be very. . ." She sighed in frustration. "Look, just because I can't think of anything right now doesn't mean Japan isn't fraught with danger." She was still clutching one of the folders, and her hands tightened around it — Carly was afraid she was going to wring its neck!

Sam had had enough. "*Ulch*, c'mon lady!" she shouted.

"It's okay," Spencer tried to reassure Mrs. Benson. "I'm goin' with 'em. So it's not like they won't have a responsible adult making sure everything goes smoothly."

Freddie nodded beside Spencer, and Carly and Sam tried to look confident as well. Mrs. Benson's frown lessened just a notch.

Unfortunately, Spencer's headlight hat chose that exact moment to burst into flames.

Everybody started screaming and gesturing. It took Spencer a second to realize why, and then he began screaming as well.

"Oh, put it out, put it out!" he pleaded. "Now! Go! Please!"

Sam grabbed a stack of hand towels from the kitchen table and tossed some to Freddie and Carly. The three of them descended upon Spencer, who was now crouching down so they could reach his flaming helmet, and they began beating the fire out. None of them were really surprised — for some reason most of Spencer's inventions burst into flames. Even the ones that had nothing to do with electricity or fire.

Finally the fire was out and Spencer sank down onto one of the stools. Then he seemed to remember that Mrs. Benson was still standing there, looking horrified.

"So," he told her more quietly, "I'll make sure everything goes smoothly in Japan." His hat was still smoking.

Mrs. Benson shook her head. "Freddie, you're not going to Japan!" she declared. She grabbed his arm and headed for the door, dragging him with her. "You're coming home with me to take a bath."

"Wait!" Carly shouted, running after them. They couldn't go without Freddie! She spit out the first idea that popped into her head. "Why don't you come to Japan with us?"

"*Aaahhh*!" Sam screamed and stepped in front of Carly.

"What?" Carly demanded.

Sam glared at her. "I don't wanna take a trip across the world with that mess of a woman!"

"C'mon, Mrs. Benson," Spencer added, crossing the room to join the rest of them. "It'll be fun." He raised a hand to his ear as if taking a call, and gasped. "What's that? I think I hear Tokyo callin' Toki-you!" He pointed at her and gave her his biggest smile.

"Come with us to Japan," Freddie urged his mom as Carly turned back to take another look at their information packets. "You love sushi!"

Mrs. Benson actually seemed to be weakening! "I suppose it would be nice to try a California roll from where it all started," she admitted.

Carly pulled the tickets out of the box. "Wait, hang on, we have a problem," she called out. She carried the tickets over to everyone else.

"What?" Spencer asked her.

"Three tickets," Carly answered, holding them up.

"Good!" Sam told her. Then she glanced back at Freddie and Mrs. Benson and shrugged. "I mean, oh no." Carly frowned, though. She knew there was no way Spencer would let her go without him, and she didn't even blame him. Three kids on their own in Japan? Not a good plan! But if Freddie couldn't go, the *iCarly* team wouldn't be complete, and that could be a disaster, too!

"Here, let me see them," Spencer told her. She handed them over and he scanned them. "Okay, great!" he assured them after a second. "These are first-class tickets! I can just trade these for five coach seats and we're all set!"

Freddie turned to his mom, pleading all over his face.

"Oh, all right!" she agreed at last. "But if we're all going to Japan, there's a lot of preparation to be done. We'll need passports, fresh underwear, a voltage converter for your night-light . . ." She took Freddie's arm and headed for the door again as Carly and Sam laughed.

"I don't need a night-light anymore!" Freddie protested. But the look on his face said he wasn't telling the truth.

"Man, she's a piece a' work," Spencer laughed after they'd gone.

Then his headlight hat began burning again.

"Put it out, put it out!" Spencer begged as Sam and Carly grabbed their hand towels a second time. "Why does this keep happening to me?"